CW01664720

# VOYAGE TO BLACKBEARD'S ISLAND

## RICK AND ROSE SINCLAIR ADVENTURE #2

RUSSELL JAMES

SEVEREDPRESS

**VOYAGE TO BLACKBEARD'S ISLAND**



**WWW.SEVEREDPRESS.COM**



***ISBN: 978-1-922861-70-2***

Dedication

*For Christy,*

*The finest treasure I have ever found.*

Other books by Russell James

<u>Rick and Rose Sinclair Adventures</u>
*Quest for the Queen's Temple*

<u>Grant Coleman Adventures</u>
*Cavern of the Damned*
*Monsters in the Clouds*
*Curse of the Viper King*
*Forest of Fire*
*Mammoth Island*
*Atoll X*
*Desolation Canyon*

<u>Ranger Kathy West National Park Adventures</u>
*Claws*
*Dragons of Kilauea*
*Ravens of Yellowstone*

# CHAPTER ONE

*1915*

Pablo raised a hand to shield his eyes from the sun's unrelenting glare. He squinted across the bow of his bobbing dory to the open Caribbean Sea.

*Yes!*

His pulse quickened. It hadn't been his imagination. In the distance, he'd spotted an island. His salvation was at hand.

Days ago, now he was unsure how many, he'd left his fishing village in his sailing dory. Money had been tight since the Great War started, and a decent catch would be enough to pay the overdue rent.

He'd been hoping for one last cast of his nets before the darkening clouds in the sky became a storm. By afternoon, a contrary wind and an outgoing tide had proved to be more than his little boat could fight. He'd gotten so far from shore that he lost sight of land. Then the great, gray clouds turned black, and the storm broke. Lightning, thunder, and lashing rain sent him cowering down by the keel, only looking up long enough to bail water from the swamping boat.

The storm passed and left a uniform gray sky behind. With no sun to orient himself, and no idea how far the storm had swept him from shore, Pablo realized he faced an almost hopeless situation. The storm had torn the mainsail, so he shortened it and set a course that maximized the wind he had available. He had no idea where he was going, but wherever it was, he might as well get there as quickly as possible.

Finally, with an island sighted, it looked like he'd gotten somewhere.

He tacked for the shore. As he closed in on the island, his hopes soared. A single, barren peak rose from an island covered in lush green. He had no idea where this island was, but he doubted that a place like this could still be uninhabited in 1915. The opening of the Panama Canal last year had turned most island real estate here into a precious commodity.

As he came within a hundred yards of shore, he could make out the narrow, white sand beach that ran like a skirt around the island. He also saw something far less welcoming. A fishing boat half buried in that brilliant sand. A big chunk had been taken out of the keel. The captain must have run her aground on a reef. Nothing that he'd ever seen in the sea would have been big enough or powerful enough to take a bite like that out of a boat.

Further north, he spied a break in the beach. Closing on it, he saw it was an entrance to a cove. Now that was a godsend. Such a place would protect him from the worst of the sea if another storm blew in. He sailed through the channel and into the bay.

Jungle ringed the cove on two sides, but straight ahead across the water rose a wall of jumbled rocks that was part of the island's central mountain. What he didn't see on any side was civilization. His hope of spying a dock with cold beer and warm food for sale nearby evaporated.

But there was evidence people had been here before. The skeleton of an old wooden sailing ship lay nose-first on the beach. The planking that had made up the outer hull was long gone, but the sturdier timbers that had supported them rose up from the sand like the ribcage of a long-dead creature. He'd seen examples like this at home, where storms scoured away sand and threw old wrecks up for all to see, at least until the sea again claimed them for its own.

He began to wonder what kind of ship this had been that had sunk in this little bay so long ago. In the days when wooden ships sailed the sea, they frequently carried treasure back from the New World to Europe. Images flashed through his mind: gold, silver, jewels. He'd heard of people finding lost treasure and becoming rich overnight. Maybe getting blown here by the storm would wind up being the best thing that ever happened to him.

All his worries about his thirst and hunger disappeared, replaced by dreams of fantastic wealth, of digging his hands in the sand and bringing up Spanish pieces of eight, of opening a chest stuffed with a rainbow of precious stones. He beached his boat to the left of the wreck and jumped over the side into calf-deep water. He had no shovel to do any proper digging, so he took what he did have with him, the paddle.

Pablo splashed his way over to the wreck and stepped into it amidships between the ribs. He still stood on sand, but if the ship's ribs were intact, they had to be attached to a keel down below. Any seaman worth his salt would store treasure down low by the keel to help keep the ship stable.

*Wouldn't it be something if a little bit of it was still there?* he thought.

The idea of being so close to fantastic wealth made him giddy. Facing the bow, he dug the sand away with the paddle, then knelt down in the water and sifted the area with his hands. Churned silt obscured his view and he searched by feel. His fingers touched something hard. He grabbed it and lifted it into the daylight.

Pablo held a cleat in his hand, about eight inches long and pretty well-preserved. He threw it up on the beach.

Not what he was looking for, but at least proof that something valuable might still be here.

He whipped around and faced the ship's missing stern. Pablo began a frantic, shoveling search of the sand at his feet, sweeping it away left and right with the paddle, working his way deeper into the water. Searching this wreck was going to change his life. He was certain of it.

Out in the bay, something splashed. He looked up, but only saw the ring of ripples left by whatever it had been. He reasoned that meant there were fish to catch here. That was good news, because if he was going to be digging up treasure, he wasn't leaving until he possessed every bit the island had to offer.

Pablo went back to work, now in water knee-deep. A memory of a picture he'd seen came back to him, a snapshot of one man's find, a gold cross with emeralds mounted in it. Oh, how he'd love to discover something like that.

Another splash sounded from in front of him, this time much closer. Again, all he saw were ripples.

He went back to work, sweeping away at the sand, his face inches from the water. Suddenly a rank odor seemed to blanket the surface of the bay. It smelled like algae and rotten fish, with a hint of sulfur. He wrinkled his nose and looked up.

Several feet away two large black bumps about a foot apart stuck out of the water. Within each, a golden eye with a vertical slit pupil looked right at him. Pablo's heart skipped a beat and he dropped his paddle. Pee warmed the water between his legs.

*Those eyes look like...but it can't be...they're so big...*

Pablo took a step back, but far too late.

In a flash, the massive head of a caiman alligator burst through the surface of the water. Its jaws opened and what looked like a hundred sharp, white, snaggled teeth gleamed in the sun. The inside of its mouth blazed sunset-red. It hissed and sent a hot putrid cloud of breath over Pablo.

Before he could react, the creature struck. Lightning fast, it lunged out of the water. The last thing Pablo felt was the slimy inside of the creature's mouth before its teeth severed his body in half.

# CHAPTER TWO

*1938*

Rick Sinclair unloaded the contents of his old Model A truck into his antique shop's storage area. The estate sale he'd attended had been for the effects of a ship's captain, and everything that had been for sale reflected a lifetime spent at sea.

Rick and his wife Rose owned the Treasure Hunters Antiques shop in Savannah, Georgia. Their forte was picking up the bargain items at estate sales and funneling them to wealthy new owners for a good profit. At least that was supposed to be their forte. The Great Depression had thrown them a curveball and over the past few years, the supply of high-end goods had exceeded demand. People worried about a roof over their head were not in a rush to have a rare painting hanging on the wall under that roof.

He wasn't thrilled with what he'd brought back today. First, he couldn't see how any of the things Rose wanted him to buy would appeal to anyone. Second, none of it had that unique element that Rick liked to find. He was a fan of the longshot purchase, the item so undervalued he could buy it cheap, and then sell it dear to the one person in the world who wanted it. He'd rather make that one big score twice a year than sell a steady stream of low margin junk all year long.

He turned to see Rose approaching. She had her red hair tied back in a ponytail and wore the long painter's smock she favored when cleaning and polishing new inventory. Her blue eyes sparkled as she saw the new items in the room and the truck half-full of goods at the dock. She wiped a bit of dirt from one of her high cheekbones.

Rick smiled. A few smudges of dirt only accentuated her fair skin.

Rose limped a bit as she crossed the room. She and Rick had had quite an adventure a few months ago. While searching for the lost temple of the Queen of Sheba, she'd been shot, and her recovery had been slow. Initial treatment in Aden had been poor, and her doctor at home had to help her fight off an infection.

"You're back late," she said.

"For the first time ever," Rick said, "there was a slow-talking auctioneer. I felt like jabbing him with a cattle prod."

"Did you get everything we wanted to bid on?"

"I got everything *you* asked me to bid on. That means I didn't bid on the great collection of creepy shrunken heads, and instead I bought this load of crap."

Rose hopped up into the truck and opened a beat-up old sea chest with LOT #26 written on it in chalk. She looked in and grinned. Rose took out an old leather-bound book and showed it to Rick.

"This 'load of crap' includes a collection of amazing first editions that the old captain collected during his travels around the world. We'll take these up to New York and make a nice profit."

"Some of the books are so old they'd fall apart if you tried to read them."

"They are far too valuable to read."

"That makes about as much sense as having clothes too valuable to wear." Rick couldn't wait another minute to tell her his next bit of news. "And speaking of valuable, I sold the polar bear."

The stuffed polar bear purchase had been one of his longshots. Rose had been furious when he'd brought it home and she'd predicted that it would never sell.

Rose's eyes narrowed. "You're kidding. To who?"

"Some guy named Willis. He also bought that painting of a ship in the Arctic you didn't want me to buy."

"Because that work was by a no-name artist," Rose said. "Someone buying that *would* buy a stupid polar bear to go alongside it. What did he pay for the bear?"

"Twice what we paid for the initial lot that included it."

Rose eyed him askance. "No one would pay that much for that stuffed bear."

"Willis couldn't resist once he heard about its storied history," Rick said. "How its meat helped a stranded whaling crew survive until rescue, and how afterwards they stuffed the skin in honor of its sacrifice."

"Do you know that's true?"

"I don't know that it isn't. The moral of the story is that Willis is happy with the bear, we're happy without the bear, and there's no harm done."

"Please leave all the selling to me in the future," Rose said. "I'd like to maintain a reputation for honesty and quality."

Rick jumped up into the truck beside Rose and picked up a framed oil painting of fruit on a table. The fruits looked partially melted.

"But you think this silly painting will wow anyone with its quality?" Rick said. "Everything in it is cock-eyed."

"People pay a lot for that artist's cock-eyed work."

Rick stepped down from the truck. He lost his footing. The painting slid from his grasp and hit the floor corner-first. The glass shattered and the frame broke in half.

"Rick!" Rose shouted.

Rick cursed himself for being so careless. He pulled the canvas from the floor and shook the glass fragments from the painted surface. He blew some remaining dust from the edges. With a penitent grin, he handed it to Rose.

"See, no harm done. I can fix that frame."

Rose took the picture. "You'd better."

Rick picked up the backing from the canvas off the floor. The side that had faced the back of the painting had an old and yellowed document attached to it. He held it under the light.

It was a hand-drawn map, done in the style of a navigation chart. It contained the outline of an island with a good-sized harbor. A sideways V in the harbor had little hash marks along its interior. Faded arrows and numbers surrounded the island. The lower right-hand corner contained a picture of a skeleton pointing an arrow at a heart. The lower lefthand corner contained a strange symbol Rick did not recognize, crescent moon with a jagged line between both endpoints. In pencil along the side, someone had printed BLACKBEARD'S ISLAND.

"Look at this," Rick said. "A chart of Blackbeard's Island. Growing up, the fishermen here used to tell stories about the pirate Blackbeard having a spot where he stored his share of the plunder, an uncharted island."

"Not really uncharted if there's a map to get to it. Probably something some kids drew up."

Rick handed her the backing board. "Look it over. Doesn't it appear to be over a hundred years old?"

Rose took the chart and gave it a close look. She squinted at it, then she took it to the work bench and inspected it through a magnifying glass.

"Well?" Rick said.

"It is on parchment," she said, "and the holes in the lettering mean the ink is probably period-correct iron-based. But just because it's old, doesn't mean that it's a legitimate map."

"But what if it is? You and I could be the ones to discover Blackbeard's treasure."

"We're not sailing around the ocean following a map we found stuck behind a painting." She tapped her healing leg. "Have you forgotten what happened looking for the Queen of Sheba's fortune?"

"I remember that we got home alive with two jewels that were worth enough to buy this building. And this time we wouldn't have to deal with any camels. Imagine what we'll find on a lost pirate island. I'm guessing a lot of treasure."

The look on Rose's face told him she was considering the idea. "I'd have to do more research on all of this. And we couldn't be away from the shop for more than a week."

"No problem. This will be a breeze. Trust me."

# CHAPTER THREE

Late the next day, Rose Sinclair locked the front door of Treasure Hunters Antiques and flipped the hanging sign around to read CLOSED. The shop was supposed to be open for another hour, but the streets of Savannah had been empty all afternoon and she didn't have any appointments scheduled. Since the onslaught of the Great Depression nine years ago, she'd found that almost all business ended up being conducted in the morning. She had better things to do than sit behind a counter or dust the rows of eclectic inventory she and her husband had on display. And one of those projects had been eating at her since yesterday.

Rose went to the storeroom in the back and flicked on the light. A jumble of crates and boxes filled most of the space, except for a narrow path to the door to the loading dock out back and a way to get to her workbench. Here was where she cleaned, repaired, and inspected some of the more interesting finds that she and her husband Rick acquired. She went to the bench, pulled her long red hair back into a ponytail, donned a set of white cloth gloves and an old painter's smock, and turned on a light over the bench.

It was time to authenticate the supposed pirate map Rick had found hidden behind the painting. She moved the protective felt-covered wooden square from the benchtop to reveal the map she'd been pressing beneath it. The sepia-toned document was about two feet long by one foot wide. The ink had faded badly, in some places to a ghostly quality. A drawing of an island covered the center of the page. The map had no scale, but from the outline it had a decent harbor tucked into a crescent of land.

The map appeared to be a genuine early 18th century work. But her experience was that appearing authentic and being authentic were two different things. Rose couldn't count the number of fake documents she'd come across. She could definitely count the number her husband had brought back to the shop, bragging that he'd gotten a true treasure at a bargain price. Many a time she'd crushed his dreams of quick riches with the invalidations she'd made at this table.

Rose took a magnifying glass to the map. From the feel and the grain, it certainly was printed on parchment. Wood pulp paper would have been a dead giveaway as a later 19th century work, and contemporary rag pulp paper could not have survived all the way to 1938. People of the times knew all too well how fragile paper was, and whoever made this map used more expensive parchment for its durability.

*Especially important in the salt air and wildly swinging temperatures of the open sea,* she thought.

Rose checked her enthusiasm, unwilling to let any wild hopes color her scientific assessment. She turned her attention to the lettering. The ink had been applied with a quill, based on the varying widths of each stroke, and not done with the kind of care professionals of the time would have used. The quality of the script was good, but by no means great. Both of those attributes might lead to her considering this a forgery.

She moved the light closer. Ink had sealed the hint of a pencil sketch beneath the outline of the island. So, one person drew the map, and then gave it over to another to do the inking.

Her comic book-obsessed husband Rick would love knowing that. This process was similar to how different comic book artists did the drawing, the ink, and the coloring. If this map was the real thing, the multi-person execution might have been for more than aesthetics. It might have been for security. The man doing the inking of a sketched map could have been told that it was fictional to keep his interest level purely professional.

A closer look at the letters revealed tiny holes burned through the parchment, consistent with the use of homemade iron gall ink. Commercial varieties were better balanced to keep the iron from oxidizing through the paper, but in Colonial America, small batches had been made locally, and generally with varying levels of quality. On this sheet, some lettering had burned through the parchment from an overabundance of iron, while other sections had faded away due to too little pigmentation. A string of numbers and circular diagrams along one side of the page were exceptionally faint. Forgers rarely faked things to this delicate a degree.

The lock on the loading dock door clicked open. The door creaked open and she looked up to see Rick step in.

She hated to admit it, but there were times he'd walk into a room and he'd still make her heart race. His strong jaw and jet-black hair with a razor part on the side gave him a matinee idol look in the right light. Someone had once mentioned he had a resemblance to Errol Flynn and he'd grown out a pencil moustache like Errol's the next week. Broad shoulders and large biceps didn't hurt his looks one bit. She wasn't the only one taken in by his charms. When he flashed his smile, he could convince most people to follow one of his impressive plans.

Impressive in the presentation, that is. In the execution, most of his plans came up a little short on actual planning, and very short on balancing risks and rewards.

"Rosie girl!" he said. "Polar bear delivery mission accomplished."

"Thank God," she sighed. "If I had to have that taxidermied animal staring down at me one more day, I was going to set it on fire."

"You're just a little jealous that I bought the bear, and found a buyer, and turned us a profit," Rick said. "And because I'm the bigger man, I'm not going to lord it over you."

"Like you're doing right now? Well, because I'm the perfect wife, I won't give you a quick review of the other worthless purchases you've made without asking me."

"Like what?"

Rose pointed to the jumble of items along the left side of the room. "Like everything over there that we've never sold."

"All those items will find a buyer. Trust me, they're unique, and appeal to only the most discerning eye. Just like what I have in the truck outside."

Rose's face flushed. "You weren't supposed to buy anything."

"Couldn't pass this one up. It'll make us a mint, trust me."

"'Trust me.' The two least favorite words I ever want to hear from you."

She followed him out the door to the loading dock. Their battered Model A Ford truck was backed up to the dock. In the bed stood an ornate, hand-carved china cabinet. Seven feet tall and four feet wide, the weight of it made the truck sag on its springs.

Rose grimaced. But before she could step forward to give it a closer inspection, the gut-churning stink of skunk enveloped her. She pinched her nose closed and stepped back.

"Damn, there's a skunk under the loading dock."

"Correction. There *was* a skunk, and it was inside the china cabinet."

Rose took another step back to try and escape the stench's invisible cloud. "Smells like it's still in there."

"Nope, double checked. See, Mr. Willis, who bought the bear, had been out of town for two weeks. When he came back, a skunk had gotten into the house and taken up residence in the china cabinet. Even had a litter of little skunks. They skedaddled when Willis returned home, but not until momma skunk left a secretion to express her displeasure. He had the cabinet taken outside and it's been airing out for about a week."

"That thing could air out for a year and still stink. Old, dry wood like that will absorb skunk spray down to its core."

"Hardly. We'll just leave it on the dock a little while longer, clean it up a bit, layer on some scented polish, and it will be right as rain."

"Clean it up with what? Gasoline and a match?"

"You might not believe this, but I got sprayed by a skunk as a kid."

"I'd certainly believe you were doing something to the skunk that made you deserve it."

Rick grimaced. "Anyway, Mom scrubbed me down with ketchup and I was clean as a whistle."

"And probably smelled like a hamburger," Rose said. "So, you're going to buy a few gallons of ketchup and treat that thing like a piece of fried liver?"

"Sure, it will be our little couple's project."

"You start slathering ketchup around in my shop and it will become a one-man project. This mess and the aftermath of its failure are one hundred percent on you. And your first step needs to be moving that thing the hell away from the loading dock. I don't want that stink around my workbench or any of the inventory that actually has value."

"If I leave it in the lot behind the shop someone might steal it."

"Never going to happen. Even the most destitute hobo would hit the soup kitchen and sleep under a newspaper before he got within ten feet of that."

"Rosie, because I'm an amazing husband, when we turn that cabinet into a pile of cash, I will not hold it against you and I'll use a part of the profits to get you that hat you admired at Harrelson's down the street."

"I'd better clean up the hat I have. It's in for a longer tour of duty."

They stepped back into the shop and Rick glanced over at Rose's work table. "You've been checking out the map?"

"Just a little."

"It's the real McCoy, isn't it?"

"Was it actually made in the 1700s?" Rose said. "I haven't found anything to say it wasn't. Is it actually a map to pirate treasure?"

"Of course it is." Rick pointed to a pentagon symbol on the island interior. "And that marks the spot."

"Shouldn't it be an X, Long John Silver?"

"Even pirates thought that was cliche."

"We'll never know for sure."

"We'll know if we try to find the island."

Rose gave him a look like he'd recommended they go wing walking on a biplane. "Pack up on an expedition to the Caribbean to sail around looking for an uncharted island based on a scrap of parchment? Not on your life."

"How else can we determine if the map is genuine?"

"Maybe start by talking with an actual Blackbeard expert, see what that person says."

"Well," Rick said, "I don't know any Blackbeard experts."

"I might. I know of a woman named Virginia Ellis who curates a pirate museum up in South Carolina. She could tell us if the whole idea of Blackbeard having a treasure island makes sense."

Rick's eyes lit up. "Great. We'll leave in the morning."

"I can call her on the phone. It's 1938, not 1908."

"This should be done in-person. I want to see if she's bluffing with what she's telling us."

"Every discussion we have with someone isn't a poker game."

"Every day of life is a poker game, Rosie. Lucky for you, I'm pretty good at it. Where is this woman?"

"Charleston."

"Let's jump in the truck and go. It will be a nice overnight get away."

"In our truck? It's more likely to be a weeklong series of walks between repair shops."

"C'mon, Rosie. It'll be fun, a short second honeymoon in genteel Charleston. Strolling along brick-paved streets in the shadows of elegant homes. It'll be a treat."

Rose pondered this plan. She didn't have client meetings lined up for the next two days. The two of them hadn't been more than a few miles from home since their return from Yemen. A change of pace would be nice, and it would be refreshing to meet another woman with an interest in history.

"Okay." Rose stepped back into the shop and pulled an old bridle from a display. She returned to the room and tossed it to Rick. "But if that truck dies along the way, I'm not walking anywhere. You're wearing this and pulling me and the truck the rest of the way to Charleston."

Rick grinned. "I'll take that bet. This trip will be a cinch."

# CHAPTER FOUR

The next day, Rick slowed the truck as soon as it crossed the Ashley River Bridge and they entered Charleston. Rose had been silent for a while and he glanced over to her.

Two of the many things Rick loved about his wife was her high cheekbones and fair complexion. Right now, that fair complexion had faded to white and the tip of her cute nose was quite red. Her eyes were an icier than normal blue and she shivered under a Great War army-surplus wool blanket.

Rick was damn near as cold as she looked. The Model A was in no way built for comfortable driving in brisk weather. Air leaked in from the gaps around the windows, the metal floor seemed to absorb the cold and radiate it back into the cabin, and while newer models had a cabin heater, this 1929 version did not. He hoped an apology might warm things up a little.

"I'm sorry this trip turned out so miserable," he said. "It was warmer when we left."

"It was Indian summer when we left." Rose's voice was as cold as she looked. "A front blew through and now it's instant winter. I should have brought warmer clothes." She sniffed at the blanket and wrinkled her nose. "This was already in the truck. What do you use it for?"

"Wrapping auction items so they don't get damaged."

"What was the last thing you wrapped in this?"

Rick hesitated. "The china cabinet."

"Ahhh!" Rose dropped the blanket. "You wrapped me in a skunk blanket?"

A shiver wracked her body. Then her teeth chattered. Rose grumbled something Rick was glad he didn't understand. She pulled the blanket off the floorboard and pulled it up to her chin. "If I stink from this thing, you'll never hear the end of it."

"A rose, wrapped by any other blanket, would smell as sweet."

"Remind me to murder you when my hands warm up enough to hold a knife."

"I'll make a note of it."

Rick realized he wasn't quite sure of where they were going in the city. He slowed the truck further. A big Buick honked behind him.

"Where do we turn?" he said.

"Here on Rutledge. Then we take it all the way to the waterfront."

Rick took a right and they passed through old Charleston. Many of the buildings looked like they'd been here since before the Civil War and the narrow street clearly had not been designed with motor cars in mind. A few minutes later, the road ended at a row of warehouses that lined the waterfront. The place had no doubt been bustling a decade ago, but the Great Depression had taken its toll. People were too poor here to buy imported items, and people overseas were too poor to pay to have things imported. Much of Charleston's seaport had become a ghost town.

"You're sure she'll be here?" Rick said.

"When I called, she said she'd be here all day. I told her we were already in town and wanted to talk about pirates. I didn't tell her your stupid poker-playing analogy."

"Even if we don't find her, this relaxing drive to Charleston was worth it."

Rose gritted her teeth. "We're looking for Warehouse 14."

A few buildings down they came to one with a big 14 painted on the side. A late model Chevrolet sedan was parked by the door. The building needed some fresh paint and the metal roof carried an unhealthy amount of rust. Rick parked next to the Chevrolet.

"I don't see a sign that this is a museum," Rick said.

"It's the right address. If it's the wrong place, whoever owns that car might tell us where the right place is."

The two of them left the truck and went to the front door. Rick expected it to be locked. After all, this wasn't the safest looking neighborhood. But the door proved to be open.

"I'll follow you," Rick said. "Ladies first, of course. Plus, you're the one she's expecting."

Rick followed Rose inside. He was not impressed.

If this was a museum, it was the worst one Rick had ever been in. The place made the storeroom in their shop look like an example of supreme organization. Most of the crap piled about looked much more like fishing gear than pirate treasures. Heavy nets lay in piles. Broken crab traps made a pyramid in the corner. The centerpiece in this homage to a failed fishing business was a wooden dory lying on its side. The bottom had rotted away and mottled black algae covered its once-white surface.

Rose made a cautious crossing of the warehouse. They got to the rear corner, and this spot was a different story. Amid a collection of much more organized crates, a small woman in a heavy jacket worked at a table under a hanging light. She wore round rimless glasses. A red headscarf tied her hair back behind her and framed a narrow face with a long nose.

"That had better be Virginia," Rose said.

The two went back to the table. The woman turned and looked them up and down. Rose smiled and approached the woman with her hand extended.

"Virginia Ellis? I'm Rose Sinclair. We spoke on the phone."

The woman smiled and revealed a set of teeth stained yellow from nicotine. Rick noted an overfilled ash tray at one corner of the table. He guessed only the draftiness of the warehouse kept the air from stinking of tobacco. The last few years, more women had started taking up smoking. He wasn't a fan of the fad, even for men.

Virginia shook Rose's hand. "Nice to meet you. I'm glad you could stop by while you were in town."

Rick didn't need the conversation to degenerate into he and Rose having to spin a fabric of lies about what they'd been doing in Charleston. To redirect things, he stepped forward and offered Virginia his hand. "I'm her husband, Rick."

They shook, but Virginia offered almost no grip. The warehouse's cold had probably chilled her hands.

"You have a reputation as an 18th century pirate expert," Rose said. "We run an antique shop in Savannah and wanted to better authenticate items people bring us claiming to be pirate-related."

"Especially interested in Blackbeard," Rick said. "People I grew up with always told me he sailed the waters around here."

"Those people were correct," Virginia said. "Captain Edward Teach, a.k.a. Blackbeard, sailed between here and the Caribbean, plundering many ships. He even had a home up in the Outer Banks of North Carolina."

"A secret pirate lair?" Rick said.

"Oh no," Virginia said. "People knew he lived there, even the governor knew it. Kind of the way drug lords live in the open in some countries today. Teach had quite a reputation in his day. He started his criminal career legitimately, sailing under another captain who was a British privateer."

"Pretend I don't know what a privateer is," Rick said.

"A privateer is, well, a legal pirate. A government gives the person the legal right to attack the shipping of a foreign power. It's the cheapest and quickest way to make a navy, but that navy isn't all that reliable, and the ethics of commissioning privateers is questionable, at the least."

"At the least," Rose said.

"In the 1700s, the Brits were at war with the French. The war concludes and all privateer licenses are revoked. But Teach and the others have been making a good living, so they all convert to piracy. Teach ends up commanding his own ship and, in 1717, transfers his command to a captured French vessel he renames *Queen Anne's Revenge*. Eventually she'd carry as many as 40 guns."

"That's a true warship at the time," Rose said. "The *U.S.S. Constitution* was rated for 44 guns."

"It gets worse than that. Soon, Teach has a fleet of several captured ships sailing with him. The fleet was strong enough to even blockade Charleston Harbor until the local government supplied the pirates with medical supplies."

"I do appreciate a man who can make that bold a bet," Rick said.

"In 1718," Virginia continued, "the king offers a pardon to all pirates who agree to go straight. Some of Teach's crews take the king up on it. Teach sails around for a bit, sees that the pardon is respected, and gets one for himself."

"It sounds like circumstance forced him into it, not his conscience."

"Indeed, that turns out to be true. He soon returns to piracy, based out of North Carolina. Eventually, the governor of Virginia sends some vessels down to take Teach off the seas for good. The *Revenge* goes aground and Teach moves to a smaller ship. The Virginia ships catch up with him, and there is a battle in November, 1718. Teach is killed. Brutally."

"Brutally?" Rose said.

"In the hand-to-hand combat aboard Teach's ship, it is reported that he was stabbed over two dozen times, and even shot, before he finally stopped fighting. The opposing commander severed the pirate's head and hung it from the bowsprit as a trophy when he sailed back into port."

"What about all the wealth Blackbeard was supposed to have amassed all those years?" Rick said.

"That's just the stuff of legends. Normally it would have been aboard the *Queen Anne's Revenge*. But plenty of reports from people who boarded the grounded ship said there weren't any valuables at all on board. There were no riches aboard the vessel he captained when he died, or buried at any of the places he lived ashore. During the time between the sinking of *Queen Anne's Revenge* and Blackbeard's last battle, the rumor was that he'd spirited away the riches to a safe place outside all legal jurisdictions."

Rick gave Rose an "I told you so" look. She ignored it.

"Has anyone found *Queen Anne's Revenge*?"

"Still lost in the shifting sands off the Carolina coast somewhere. And Blackbeard's supposed horde of riches has never been found, or even verified to have ever existed."

"His crew would have known where it was," Rick said. "I mean, he wouldn't have buried it by himself."

"And there's a great tall tale about why. The story is that back when Blackbeard began his pirate career, he enlisted the help of a witch, who cast a spell of success over him. That would account for his rapid rise to command of vessels and even a fleet, as well as his ability to elude pirate hunters at almost every turn. The belief that he was protected by magic was validated by the near impossibility of killing him during his final battle. The conquering captain beheaded him afterwards believing that only decapitation could break the spell the witch cast."

Rick was a bit dubious of this whole witchcraft angle. "You're saying the sailors wouldn't go find the gold because of some kind of magic protection?"

"Ghostly protection," Virginia said. "The story was that Blackbeard had the witch with him on the journey to hide the treasure. She cast a particularly powerful hiding and protection spell on the location. Then Teach killed her so she could never revoke it. The spirit of the dead witch turned the entire island against him and his men."

"That sounds outlandish," Rose said.

"All myths usually are," Virginia said. "But it is true that in his last voyage before his death, Teach set sail from North Carolina with full crews aboard two ships, and returned with a skeleton crew manning one."

"That could have been the result of failed pirate raids," Rick said.

"Teach's pirate raids never failed."

Rose pulled some pieces of vellum paper from her pocket and set them on the table. She showed the first one to Virginia. It was a tracing of the skeleton pointing a giant arrow at a heart that had been at the corner of the map.

"Does this symbol mean anything to you?" Rose said.

Virginia's eyes widened. "Where did you find this?"

"On an old document purportedly tied to Blackbeard."

"If it dates to the right period, it certainly was related to Blackbeard. This is the image he used on many documents. He could read and write, but he used this to impress those who did not. It was also on the flag he flew on his ships, one of the first openly recognized pirate flags."

"So far, the document seems to check out. The material and inks are period correct. What do you make of this?" Rose showed her another page that contained tracings of the strange numbers and circles beside the map.

"Oh, now that is interesting," Virginia said. "Notations like this were used on nautical charts. Not professional ones, but ones that might be used by those who could not read. These circles and crescents are phases of the moon and the numbers are depths in fathoms. The inverted brackets around them all indicate a narrow passage. This would be used to let sailors know the high tide depth of a pass on a maritime chart."

Virginia's eyes widened as she saw the last symbol Rose had copied over, the crescent moon with a jagged line between both endpoints from the map's corner. "What kind of document did you find all these on?"

Rick cut off Rose before she could answer. "These were on separate documents. They all came in a bundle from an estate. Some of them are just fragments now."

"Ah, yes," Virginia sighed. "The tragedy of poor conservation. So many things decay so quickly, even parchment. Did you bring them with you?"

"No," Rick said. "Like you said, it's all about conservation and there was already too much damage."

"I'd love to travel down to Savannah to see them."

Rick thought the woman could not have been more obviously fishing for an invitation. Sometimes when he was in the middle of a poker game, an alarm would sound in his head that one of the players wasn't dealing from the top of the deck. That bell was starting to ring.

"That would be lovely." Rose handed her a business card from the antique shop. "Let us know when you'll be in the area."

"I will."

"Thank you for your help, Virginia," Rick said. "We'll let you get back to your work."

Rose gave Rick a quizzical look and then followed him out of the warehouse.

"What's the hurry?" she said.

"Didn't you say this warehouse was a museum?"

"I'd seen it mentioned that way in a magazine article."

"And it didn't seem a little un-museum-like to you?" Rick said.

"Maybe she is trying to get it off the ground and she embellished the description a bit for some publicity. We could have kept talking with her. She was obviously knowledgeable and there's no telling what other pirate facts she might have shared if we kept chatting."

"And there's no telling how many more details about the map she might have gotten from us." Rick shook his head. "I don't trust her."

"She's a history researcher. They don't come more harmless. You're a little paranoid."

"The harmless researchers are the worst at hiding their tells. I could see the pulse in the veins of her neck speed up when she saw the things you showed her. And she said the document we had was on parchment. We never told her that."

"She probably just guessed that," Rose said.

"You told me parchment use was rare, so that would have been a damn good guess. I know a potential weasel when I see one, and that woman had weasel written all over her."

"You deal with too many shady people, so you assume everyone is."

"And I'm usually right," Rick said.

"Now I'm not in the mood to stay here tonight," Rose said. "Let's get back home."

"I agree. We need to really inspect that map."

A gust of cold wind blew in off the harbor and made the sleeves of Rick's shirt flap. Rose shivered.

"One thing we are definitely doing before we head back." Rose went to the passenger door, picked up the skunk-scented blanket with two fingers, and threw it on the ground. "We're buying a decent blanket."

Virginia Ellis peered out of the crack between the big warehouse door and the frame. Rick and Rose Sinclair stood by the bed of an old Model A pickup. She couldn't quite hear what they were talking about, but the discussion was certainly more intense than certifying a simple document would warrant. Rick had seemed evasive in their conversation. Virginia had a pretty good idea why. Enrico Lasorda would want to know about it.

Enrico Lasorda ran most of the black-market businesses in Charleston. One of them was a trucking company that seemed to experience some inventory shrinkage with every delivery, and those stolen goods ended up all over the southeast.

Lasorda had met with Virginia personally, and unannounced, at the warehouse with what he considered a magnanimous deal. In return for "protection" she did not need, she would give him unrestricted and uninvestigated nighttime use of her warehouse. She assumed it was for transshipping stolen goods, but she was smart enough to not ask. Lasorda knew how to pick his targets. As a single female with no friends in high places, she was in no position to decline this "offer." She just moved all her important pieces to one corner, agreed, and counted herself lucky she hadn't just been killed outright.

During that conversation, he'd shown more than a casual interest in her pirate artifacts, said that he'd admired men like that, wondered what it had been like to be surrounded by treasures like the pirates had. Having seen her research, he added another condition to his deal, that she continue her work at his expense, with any leads on pirate treasure going straight to him.

The Sinclairs' visit had just solved his greed and her personal quest.

She went back to her workbench and dialed the phone. A gruff-sounding man picked up on the other end.

"Mr. Lasorda, this is Virginia."

"There better not be a problem with my warehouse."

She gritted her teeth at how he assumed the place was *his* warehouse. "No, the warehouse is fine. I got a line on something that I'm sure would interest you and make you richer."

"I'm listening, but it better be good,"

"The rumor has always been that Blackbeard left a map to the treasure he hid before he was killed. A couple from Savannah found that map."

"They showed it to you?"

"No, but from the things they described to me, they were talking about the map."

"Who are these people?"

"Rick and Rose Sinclair, antiques dealers."

"They know what they have?"

"They were pretty cagey about it," Virginia said, "so I'd say yes."

"I want that map."

"I don't know where they have it. I thought you'd have people who could take care of that kind of thing. But once you get it, I will be able to read it and interpret it for you."

"My people are a blunt force. First, I try finesse. They already trust you. Exploit that trust."

“This treasure would be priceless,” Virginia said. “Enough to buy me out of our bargain, don’t you think?”

“Call me when you have the map.”

Lasorda hung up. Virginia sighed. This plan had totally backfired. Instead of getting her a look at the Sinclairs’ map and off Lasorda’s hook, the plan had gotten the hook dug in even deeper. She wasn’t just giving the keys to her warehouse to criminals anymore. Now she was actively spying for one. Getting involved with Lasorda was like getting into quicksand. The more you struggled to get out, the deeper into it you sank.

If the Sinclairs had a map, they were certain to follow it. If she was going to get more involved, she might as well go all the way, and get the Sinclairs to take her with them.

# CHAPTER FIVE

The next morning, Rose sat at her worktable inspecting the parchment from both sides. She alternated lighting it from the front and then the rear, trying to tease as much of the faded inscriptions from the sheepskin as she could.

From the store, she heard the bell on the front door ring. Out of habit she rose to answer it, then remembered that Rick was covering the shop while she worked back here. He didn't care much for dealing with casual shoppers, so tending shop proved his commitment to getting her to uncover all the map's secrets.

A minute later Rick came back carrying a steaming cup of coffee. He set it on the workbench edge, far from the map, just where she was about to tell him to.

"Aren't you thoughtful?" she said.

"Just keeping the wheels of progress turning. How's it going?"

"Pretty good. I think I've teased out the latitude and longitude of the island, or at least what Blackbeard thought it was. Some of those coordinates were known to be horribly imprecise. And that's if I guessed properly whether some fuzzy numbers are eights, nines, or sixes."

"That's good," said a voice on the other side of the doorway. "I fly better when I have a destination before I take off."

Into the shop stepped Humphrey Custis. Rose immediately knew why Rick had been buttering her up with hot coffee. Humphrey was a well-known smuggler who barely concealed his activities under the guise of legitimate importing and exporting. Just the kind of friend Rick usually had, and just the kind of person Rose wanted to have little to do with.

Twenty years ago, he'd been a decorated, dashing Great War fighter ace. You wouldn't know it now. He wore an ill-fitting shirt that stretched over his potbelly. The coming and going of Prohibition hadn't slowed his drinking down and he had a round face and a veiny, swollen nose. He flicked a few strands of prematurely graying hair away from his face, and grinned at Rose.

"Dear Rose, always a pleasure to renew your acquaintance."

Rose rolled her eyes at what Humphrey thought passed for Southern charm. It had been a while since he'd flown them to Yemen where they'd barely escaped with their lives after finding the lost temple of the Queen of Sheba. Humphrey had definitely saved their butts that time, but that didn't make her any more comfortable with Humphrey's shoestring planning that made it happen.

"You brought Humphrey in on this?" she said to her husband.

"Well, we aren't going to swim to the island, are we? Humphrey has transportation connections."

"The booking agent for White Star Lines has transportation connections. Humphrey works with smugglers."

"Now, Rose," Humphrey said. "Your words wound me most deeply."

"Rosie," Rick said, "we can't just rent a boat and sail out there. We don't know anything about sailing. And we can't hire a commercial crew. We couldn't trust them."

"But we can trust the kind of people Humphrey deals with?"

"Now, now," Humphrey said, "I wouldn't put y'all at risk. I'd only recruit top shelf people."

"The funny thing is," Rose said, "that top shelf smugglers are still bottom of the barrel."

Rick stepped between Rose and Humphrey. "Let's make a plan. We'll see what Humphrey can do to help us, okay?"

"Okay." Rose slid a piece of paper and a current world map from one of her National Geographic magazines over to Humphrey. "These are the coordinates."

Humphrey read the coordinates and then ran two fingers down the latitude and longitude lines until they met at an empty space in the Caribbean Sea. "Ain't nothing there."

"The definition of an uncharted island," Rose said.

"Ha, ha. Makes sense though. This spot is outside the currents and trade winds that sailors favor to make their trips quicker. Commercial shipping would never have a reason to cross this stretch of ocean." He rubbed his chin. "Tell y'all what. I'll fly us down to New Orleans. I got a friend there, a Cajun boy with a fishing trawler. Has a good crew that still brings in island rum and cigars on the sly to avoid all them import duties. They'll drop us right where we need to go."

"And what will your Cajun pals want for their services?" Rose said.

"Why, a fair amount to cover expenses and such. I'll split my cut with them. But truth be told, they'll be more interested in the adventure. These are the kinda folks who wrestle snapping turtles for the hell of it."

"See," Rick said, "did I say the man was a wizard with transportation? Trust me."

Rose knew she'd been outmaneuvered, but to be truthful, Humphrey was the best person for this job, and they couldn't very well fill the cargo hold of a regular boat for hire with pirate treasure and hope to not be betrayed by strangers.

"You go get your Cajun pals on board, Humphrey." Rose turned to Rick. "And you go mind the store. We need to sell some things to pay for the gas in Humphrey's flying death trap."

"Not enough you hurt my feelings," Humphrey said, "but now you have to disparage my aircraft?"

Rick leaned over and kissed Rose's cheek, which she accepted with feigned indifference. Humphrey gave the two of them a sloppy salute and departed.

The phone on Rose's table rang. She answered it.

"Rose, this is Virginia Ellis."

"Say, Virginia." Rose didn't like that she was getting a follow up call from Virginia. She held the receiver so she and Rick could both hear the conversation. "What can I do for you?"

"It's what I'd like to do for you. I'd like to be more help on your Blackbeard project."

"You've already done quite a lot."

"I think I can help you when you start following the map."

Rose's heart leapt into her throat. She and Rick exchanged panicked looks.

*Bluff her,* Rick mouthed.

"What map?" Rose said.

"Don't kid a kidder, Rose. You've found Blackbeard's map. Once you get to the island, you'll need someone who knows Teach inside and out to help you find where a man like him would hide his treasure. There won't be a big X painted in the sand somewhere."

"Because it's under a pentagon," Rick whispered.

Rose rolled her eyes and covered the receiver. "Now what?" she said to Rick.

"Lie," Rick said. "Tell her we don't have the map."

"I'm a terrible liar. She knows we have the map."

"If we leave her here, she'll tell God-knows-who about it and we may have an unwelcome surprise waiting for us when we get back."

"Virginia may be right," Rose said. "She would probably be helpful interpreting whatever we came across. And if Virginia is with us, she can't tell others about the map."

"Hello?" Virginia said. "Are you there, Rose?"

"Fine," Rick whispered. "Match her bet, then raise. Tell her to come now."

Rose uncovered the receiver. "You'd probably be a big help, Virginia. But we're leaving tomorrow so I doubt you can make it."

"Of course I can. I'll leave here first thing in the morning."

"Okay, meet us at an old airfield twenty miles south of Savannah on the Richmond Hill Road at noon."

"Will do." Virginia hung up.

Rick patted Rose on the shoulder. "Look at you, playing poker like a pro."

"That conversation was strange."

"Strange as hell. And she had no problem dropping everything at a moment's notice, and didn't ask for any details about where we might be going or what to bring. She was desperate to be in on following that map."

"Blackbeard *is* her passion," Rose said. "Maybe she thinks it's the chance of a lifetime. I know how hard it is for a woman to be taken seriously. She couldn't pass up the kind of opportunity a man would take for granted."

"That wasn't the sound of a woman excited for a historical discovery. That sounded like a woman whose life depended on getting in on our trip."

Rose tried to keep from being sucked into Rick's vortex of paranoia. "So what do we do?"

“We keep playing until she lays some more cards on the table,” Rick said. “And since we’re the pit boss, we can end the game any time.”

# CHAPTER SIX

The next day, Rick stood at the tail of Humphrey's Ford Tri-Motor. The boxy plane had a wide overhead wing that supported an engine on either side. One more engine in the nose gave the aircraft its name. Splotches of green and black algae bloomed along the fuselage and the tail numbers were faded to near-indecipherability. The aircraft was never going to pass for a commercial passenger plane, or even a flyable airplane at all. That made it perfect for the kind of shadowy cargo runs Humphrey made a living doing.

Rose walked up to Rick carrying her last small bag from the Model A. "I feel like flying in this deathtrap is like betting my life on a roll of the dice. The fact that we both survived it last time makes me even more certain that we won't this time."

"Are you forgetting that I'll be right up there, co-pilot extraordinaire?"

"Yes, having an unlicensed co-pilot allays all my fears about this flying collection of worn-out parts."

"Humphrey flies the thing all the time and it always gets him home. He lets the outside look bad on purpose. But all the mechanicals under the skin are first-rate."

"How would you know? Suddenly you're a mechanic *and* a co-pilot?"

"Trust me. It's a mechanically new airplane. You can wager the bankroll on it."

The Chevrolet Rick had seen outside the Charleston warehouse entered the poor excuse for an airport. It parked by the abandoned control tower and Virginia Ellis stepped out. She was dressed in a skirt and jacket, an outfit for the kind of air travel one experienced on far better planes than Humphrey's. She looked confused and ill at ease.

"Behold," Rick said, "the expert we will rely upon has arrived."

"You can't blame her for looking confused," Rose said. "Nothing about this rundown place says there is any active aviation going on here."

Rick waved at Virginia. She waved back and came over. Her heels dug into the soft ground and she wobbled with each step.

Virginia stopped beside Rick and Rose. "I was afraid I'd made a wrong turn somewhere."

"No, this is the place." Rick patted the tail of the Tri-Motor. "And this is the plane."

Virginia raised an eyebrow. "I see. Well, where exactly will this plane be taking us? Not far, I hope."

"Bayou St. Therese, a little town north of New Orleans. Just a few hours flight."

"That's a relief. Let me get my bag." Virginia headed back to the trunk of her car.

"She should have brought her bag with her when she walked over," Rick said. "We don't need someone who can't plan even one step ahead."

"Give the poor woman a break," Rose said. "Your suspicious nature is showing."

"When my suspicious nature is your salvation, I will gladly accept your apology."

Virginia fiddled around in her trunk, then pulled out a small bag. She made her way back over to the plane, looking more relaxed. "Okay, let's go to Louisiana."

The three of them climbed up into the plane. The Tri-Motor's cabin was a no-frills affair with steel walls and a wooden floor that Rick had to admit looked just a bit rotted. Four wicker seats were bolted to the floor behind the cockpit. The air contained an unsettling aroma, a mélange of oil, gasoline, and spilled smuggled rum.

Humphrey stood in the cabin. He eyed Virginia up and down. "Y'all told me the third person was a historian."

"Virginia is a historian," Rose said, "a pirate expert."

Humphrey smiled and shrugged. "All righty, then. Well, shiver my timbers and off we go."

Rick followed Humphrey forward to take the co-pilot's seat. Rose was right that he didn't have any actual certification to fly, but Humphrey had taught him enough of the basics that he could be useful on longer flights.

Humphrey threw some switches, eased back the mixture ratio lever, and pressed the button for the center engine's starter. The propellers began a slow, halting revolution. The second cycle was even slower than the first. Suddenly, a loud boom shook the aircraft's nose. A cloud of black, oily smoke rolled over the cockpit windows. It dissipated to reveal a disc of whirling propellers.

Rick exhaled. He'd never admit it to Rose, but his confidence in Humphrey's plane wasn't as strong as he professed it to be. Honestly, he considered every mechanical function that occurred properly to be a minor miracle.

Humphrey leaned over to Rick. "You sure about that woman back yonder?"

Rick looked back at Virginia as Rose helped her with her seatbelt. "I'm never sure about anybody."

"Excepting yours truly, of course."

"Oh, I haven't been sure about you for years."

Once the plane was in level flight, the engines kicked back to a lower speed and Rose could hear herself think again. Virginia had been gripping her seat's armrests for dear life since takeoff. As the cabin grew quieter, her fingers relaxed, but the rest of her body remained rigid.

"Flying in this plane isn't as scary as it seems," Rose said, trying to relax her. She was glad Rick couldn't hear her defending Humphrey's plane. "I've done it before and I've survived,"

"I've never been in any plane before."

"Then after this one, the rest of your flights will be a breeze."

Virginia grinned, though the stains on her teeth substantially dimmed her smile. "So where is it your pirate map is going to take us?"

Rose took a large folded sheet of paper from her bag. She unfolded it to reveal a detailed tracing of the original map, then passed the tracing to Virginia. Virginia gave it a most intense inspection as Rose explained the parts of it that she understood.

"This is remarkable," Virginia said. "This is an exact duplicate?"

"I even copied over the things I didn't understand. There's this pentagon here on the island, that sideways V in the harbor, and this diagram in the corner opposite Blackbeard's skeleton and spear logo."

"Yes, some things we'll never understand. Maybe they were inside jokes to pirates. You checked the coordinates on a current map?"

"They show an empty spot in the Caribbean Sea."

"Then the island has remained undiscovered," Virginia said. "The fact that there is a longitude confirms that the map was likely Blackbeard's. At the time, longitude was difficult to calculate unless you had a very accurate timepiece. On one of Blackbeard's early raids, the prize ship had a German clockmaker as one of the passengers. Blackbeard convinced the man to join his crew at double share, as long as he could keep the ship on correct time for the purpose of navigation. The man agreed, though he may not have been given much of a choice. But having the correct time gave Blackbeard a navigation advantage that many times kept him from capture."

All the things Virginia was telling Rose made her even more confident that at least the map was real. Whether they would find the island was another story. She kept thinking *big ocean, small speck of land.* They could easily sail right past it. Maybe they'd find it, but one of the dozens of hurricanes over the last hundred years or so had swept away any remnants of Blackbeard.

She wondered if her husband had calculated their odds of success on finding the island.

Of course first, they had to find this Cajun fisherman somewhere in a Louisiana swamp.

# CHAPTER SEVEN

A few hours later, Rick did his best to keep the plane straight and level while Humphrey took care of the navigation duties. Humphrey's focus darted between the endless forested swampland out the pilot's side window and the faded map in his lap. Humphrey wasn't inspiring Rick's confidence.

"You sure you know where we are?" Rick said.

"Absolutely! In fact..." Humphrey took a long look down at the ground. "That there's the spot we're looking for. I got the controls."

Humphrey yanked at the yoke and mashed on one of the pedals. Rick let both loose and grabbed his seat as the plane went into a steep right bank. Even over the roar of the engines, Rick heard a pair of shouts of alarm from the passenger cabin. He turned to see Virginia and Rose bracing themselves against the bulkhead for support. He gave Rose a weak smile and a thumbs-up. She returned an icy stare that said "What the hell have you gotten us into?"

Rick turned around just as Humphrey leveled out and nosed the plane into a dive. Rick gripped the control panel with both hands as they closed on the treetops.

Suddenly, like the Red Sea before Moses, the trees seemed to part and reveal a strip of gravel runway. But that only made Rick's heart beat even faster. By his estimation, the clearing around it was too narrow for the wings and too short for the brakes. He knew that if he and Rose died like this, her ghost would spend eternity tormenting his ghost all around this little patch of ground.

At what seemed like at least a minute too late, Humphrey cut back the engines, deployed the flaps, and flared the aircraft's nose up. It leveled and all three wheels hit the ground at once. Through a combination of braking and engine adjustments that frankly seemed like magic to Rick, Humphrey brought the plane to a skidding halt. The plane had three feet to spare before the main propeller would have windmilled into a huge live oak at the clearing's edge.

Humphrey cut the engines. "See, now? What did I tell y'all? Easy as falling off a log."

Rick unbuckled and went back to Rose's seat. "See, now that wasn't so---"

Rose cut him off with a finger in his face. "Shut up and get me off this stupid plane."

Rick opened the rear door and jumped out. He helped Rose and Virginia down. Humphrey passed down the luggage and was the last one out.

While this area seemed like an uninhabited, swampy forest from the air, looking at it from ground level revealed something quite different. Under cover of the trees, two one-story buildings bracketed a dock that stretched out into a tree-obscured bayou. The flat roofs of the buildings hosted an array of small bushes to make the structures completely invisible from above. At the end of the dock, a rusty old shrimp boat bumped against the pilings.

"Welcome to the Beaulieu homestead," Humphrey said.

"It has all the charm of an abandoned factory," Rose said.

"Don't let the looks fool you none. Them Beaulieu boys are the best at what they do."

"Which is what, exactly?"

"Oh, little of this, little of that."

Rose turned to Rick. "And none of it legal. You introduce me to only the most elite segment of society."

"I know," Rick said. "You're so lucky. It's like you married into royalty."

"Let's go meet Damien," Humphrey said.

Everyone grabbed their bags and Humphrey led them down to the dock between the two buildings. A stout man wearing the lower half of a seaman's rain suit and a pair of boots leaned against one of the buildings. He finished hand rolling a cigarette, placed it between his lips, and then intercepted them at the foot of the dock. His hair was a mess and his smile revealed wide gaps between his teeth.

"*Fren* Humphrey, you are late." The man's Cajun accent was thick as swamp water.

"Headwinds are murder."

"You're just in time. Another hour and we would miss high tide and have to wait." Damien looked over at the other three people. "And who's this you bring with you?"

"Rick and Rose Sinclair, who are running this here show, and that's Virginia Ellis, the Blackbeard expert."

"*Bonjour mes amis*." He went straight to Rose and took her hand in both of his. "*Rouge* hair, like fire. You are even prettier than Humphrey said."

Rose shook her head. Rick knew how much it irritated her when men led a conversation by complimenting her appearance. She took it as demeaning. She never seemed to understand how strikingly attractive she was.

"That boat down there," Rose said as she withdrew her hand from his, "it's safe to take out in the ocean?"

"*Oui*. My *bâteau* is ready for the trip. The outside, she is rusty to avoid attention. But inside, she is beautiful. Her heart beats strong and hard."

Rose turned to Rick. "Just the way you described the flying rattletrap we came here in. Now I'm completely carefree."

"Business first, of course." Damien turned to Humphrey. "There is a matter of payment for my splendid services."

Humphrey pulled out a bulging envelope and handed it to Damien. "What we agreed on, plus your cut of the treasure we find."

Damien shoved the envelope into his pocket. "And this is not refundable if your island isn't where you say it is. *Allons-y!*"

Damien walked them down the dock. The closer they got, the worse the old shrimper looked. Cracks glazed the windows in the pilothouse. Varnish peeled from the weathered wooden surfaces. Dead, black algae plagued the nets draped across the stern. In his head, Rick could hear Rose telling him they were all going to drown at sea in this thing.

The crew was no more inspiring. One man lounged at the bow, and one leaned in the pilothouse doorway. Both were grizzled, unshaven, and wore ratty clothes.

Rose turned to Rick. "Are we searching for dead pirates or sailing with live ones?"

Damien barked out orders in what sounded like a guttural version of French. The two men jumped up and rushed to where the bow and stern lines were cleated to the dock. Damien led the four visitors up a gangplank to a wide hatch in the middle of the deck. Steps led down into the hold.

"Put your bags down there," he said. "There are bunks for sleeping. One of you has our destination for me?"

Rose fished a piece of paper from her pocket and handed Damien the coordinates. He looked them over and smiled.

"All right then. *Laissez les bon temps rouler!"*

"What does that mean?" Virginia said.

Damien smiled. "Let the good times roll!"

As the others took their bags below, Rick held Humphrey back. "Humphrey, you've done your part, got us here and got us a boat. I know that you don't like leaving your plane unattended in a strange place. You don't need to go to the island. Your cut will be the same."

"Are you fooling me? Damien is leaving a man back to watch the plane and the dock, so ain't no worries there. And do you think I'd let the two of you go off alone without my personal protection? Why, you wouldn't last five minutes."

"I have no idea what we'll find out there, if anything."

Humphrey slapped him on the shoulder. "That's what makes it fun! Now let's go check into our staterooms."

# CHAPTER EIGHT

"That's the place, boss," the pilot called back from the cockpit.

Enrico Lasorda looked out the window of his new Beechcraft Model 18. He'd just bought the plane a month ago, specifically for trips like this. His criminal empire was growing, and he needed a way to quickly get to any part of it. The sleek, speedy twin-engine plane was perfect for that, and the cabin had room for him to bring muscle if needed. For this trip, it was needed, and three of the seats around him were filled with bulky henchmen packing heat. He was prepared for whatever waited down in the bayou.

Being prepared was one of the traits that had made him successful. He could also see the angles no one else did, could sort out the weak from the strong by the look in their eyes, could smell a rat a mile away. Yet plenty of bosses had dismissed him, until he in turn became their boss.

His move from New York to the southeast had been a perfect example. While the crime families duked it out over city blocks, he'd seen the coast between Charleston and Jacksonville as ripe for the taking with little opposition. He'd moved south with a handpicked crew and wiped out or absorbed the local gangs in a matter of months. All the nooks and crannies along the coast had made the place a smuggler's dream for centuries, and that was still true. And the best part was that he now supplied all the warring factions in the East Coast cities, the same people who said he was stupid for heading south.

Lasorda was determined to prove them wrong again when it came to pirate treasure, the ultimate untaxable, untraceable windfall. They'd laughed at him for financing Virginia. He'd see how hard they were laughing when that investment paid off.

Down below a clearing came into view. An unimproved runway ran the length of it and near one end sat a dilapidated Ford Tri-Motor. He didn't need to read the faded tail numbers to know it was Humphrey Custis' ratty plane. How many Tri-Motors could there be sitting around Louisiana bayous?

Virginia Ellis had played her role well so far, even better than he'd expected. She not only had gotten her hands on the Blackbeard map, she'd wrangled herself a seat on the expedition the Sinclairs had launched to re-discover the lost island. Lasorda was impressed. Not enough to let her stop being the cover story for his warehouse operation, but impressed.

Virginia had left a note in the empty trunk of her car with this, the Sinclairs' intermediate location on it. The seclusion that Humphrey prized for his home town airport worked just as well in Lasorda's favor when he landed there after Humphrey had departed. No one had seen him arrive, no one had seen him search Virginia's car, and no one had seen him take off headed for Louisiana.

As Lasorda's aircraft passed over the runway, a man came out to the edge of the clearing and looked up at the plane. Then he dashed back under the cover of the trees.

"Someone's there to greet us," Lasorda said. "How nice." He shouted to the pilot, "Land the plane."

The plane made a hard corkscrew approach and the pilot brought it down on the gravel strip in the clearing's center. Only after it braked to a stop could Lasorda see that there were two buildings and a dock close to the clearing. A lifetime of experience told him that a place this secluded and rundown could only exist for illegal pursuits.

"Sal, Frankie," Lasorda said. "Get your persuaders."

The two men nodded. Lasorda left his seat and went to the cabin door. He opened it and a set of steps unfolded to the ground. A wall of hot, humid air slapped him in the face and a stench of decay that made Carolina swamps seem scented practically made his nostril hairs curl.

"What kind of inbred yokels choose to live out here?" he said.

The man he'd seen from the plane came out of one of the buildings at a run. His oversized ears stuck out from under a frayed flat cap like the handles of a jug. Lasorda noted that he ran quite well for a man with no shoes. He held a large caliber shotgun and had it pointed in Lasorda's general direction.

Lasorda descended the steps and sauntered about ten yards in front of the nose of the plane before stopping.

The yokel paused within shotgun range of Lasorda. His labored breathing made the gun barrel wave up and down with each breath.

"You can't land here," he said. "This here's private property."

Lasorda had stared down gun barrels so often the act came naturally. He took a cigar from the breast pocket of his suit coat and tucked it in the corner of his mouth.

"My name's Enrico Lasorda," he said. "You know who I am?"

"No but I know you're gonna be a corpse if'n you don't get back on that aeroplane."

"You're feisty, huh? I hate feisty. Look, I don't care about you, or this ramshackle monument to Louisiana architecture. I'm looking for the people who came in on that Tri-Motor."

"They done left in the shrimper. Long time ago."

"You're going to tell me where they went."

"No, I ain't. And if'n you don't beat it, this here shotgun's going to ventilate you."

"I have two associates who bet me that they could pull their triggers long before you could pull yours."

The yokel looked around and noticed Sal and Frankie standing one at each wingtip, and each carrying a tommy gun pointed his way. The man's eyes went wide and his shaking got worse.

Lasorda took two steps forward. "I'll say it again. I don't give a damn about you and whatever nickel-and-dime sideshow you're running in this godforsaken swamp. All I need to know is where the people who arrived in that plane sailed off to."

Lasorda could tell when a guy across from him knew he was in over his head, and this little crawdad-eating loser was way past that. The man pointed his shotgun down at the ground.

"They went to some island."

Lasorda sighed at how time-consuming it was to deal with stupid people. "Which island?"

"Didn't have a name, just a latitude and longitude. It's written on the chart on the desk in the house."

"Why did that have to take so long?" Lasorda said.

He raised two fingers in the air. The two men who flanked him opened fire. A spray of bullets shredded the yokel so badly that his jerking corpse hit the ground in three pieces.

"Go in there," Lasorda said. "Get me those coordinates."

The men advanced on the main building, weapons at the ready in case anyone else was here and feeling heroic. Lasorda wasn't worried. He figured if there was anyone else, they would have either already been out backing the now-dead yokel's play or bolted for the safety of the bayou.

Once he had the coordinates of the island, Lasorda would have the pilot hop over to New Orleans. One of his connections there could get him a boat, and his man Charlie could put his bootlegging experience to good use piloting them to the island, maybe even get there before whatever rusting hulk left this place arrived. He would leave the island with treasure. No one else would leave the island at all, including Virginia, whose usefulness, he now decided, would at that point be at an end. He did not like leaving loose ends.

He shouted to his henchmen as they entered the building. "And on the way out, burn the place to the ground."

# CHAPTER NINE

Rose stood near the bow of the boat as it rolled through the choppy Caribbean waters. Three of the four crewmen of the shrimper were downstairs playing poker with Rick. She couldn't stand it below decks. Between the rolling of the ship and the engine fumes from the old diesel, she swung between passing out and throwing up. Up here in the fresher air, the heaving ship kept her throwing up as a likely event, but she could do that over the side of the boat instead of on her own clothes.

Virginia stood back at the stern. She'd changed into more practical travelling clothes and now leaned on the stern railing, looking exactly as green around the gills as Rose felt. An unlit cigarette dangled from her lips, as if she'd thought it would help her situation, then decided against it. Rose wasn't happy the woman felt ill, but she was happy her own suffering wasn't the result of some personal weakness.

Virginia had kept to herself since the boat had worked its way down the bayou and out into the sea. Rose could not blame her for wanting to stand apart. Everything happening was a bit overwhelming.

Rick came up on deck and went to Rose's side.

"Did you run out of money?" Rose said.

Rick patted a bulging pocket. "Nope. They did."

"Did any of them speak understandable English?"

"No, but all spoke the international language of five-card-draw. I just spoke it better than they did."

"Not worried about them throwing you overboard for revenge?" Rose said.

"Before we've even gotten to the island? Never."

"How about after?"

Rick thought about it for a moment. "I may let them win the next few hands. Just to keep it friendly."

The crewman up in the crow's nest on the ship's single mast shouted something in excited Cajun. Rose turned to see Damien looking past her to the horizon using a pair of binoculars. Smoke drifted up from one of his hand-rolled cigarettes at his lips. Then the engines revved up to full speed and the ship turned slightly to starboard.

"They must see something," Rose said.

A moment later, Rick pointed off the bow. "I think we've found ourselves an island."

A low, dark lump appeared just ahead. In a short time, the boat came close enough to see the details. The island was a few miles long and rose to a barren peak hundreds of feet tall near the center. Waves lapped at a fringe of white beach. Beyond that, palm trees, ferns, and other tropical plants covered the ground. Damien shouted for Rick and Rose to come back to the pilothouse. They arrived and Humphrey stood beside the captain, balanced on one foot.

"What's with the flamingo impression?" Rick said.

"I fell belowdecks when the boat rolled. Done something nasty to my ankle."

"He can fly like a bird, but the man he has no sea legs." Damien pointed out the window. "This is your island? It is only a few miles from the spot you told me, so this must be it."

"You can thank a German watchmaker for that," Rose said.

"Now where do we go ashore?" Damien said.

Rose pulled out her copy of the map and pointed at the cove on the western side of the island. "We should anchor in here. It will be sheltered and calm."

Damien checked his compass, swung the boat more to starboard, and began to follow the coastline south.

Minutes later, the channel to the cove appeared. Within the cove, calmer water beckoned to them. Damien piloted the boat through the narrow opening. Virginia came in from the stern on decidedly unsteady legs.

As they cleared the entrance, Rose looked again at her map. She didn't like what she saw.

"Damien, stop the boat."

Damien gave the ship a quick burst of reverse. The boat stopped in a frothy churn of seawater and Damien moved the controls to idle.

"What is it?"

The map showed the cove as a rough big circle. What they were in looked more like a backwards letter D. Both sides had curving white sand beaches backed up by a palm forest. But then there was a wall of boulders straight ahead of them that bisected what would have been the circular cove. The boulders stretched up and back into the mountain that dominated the island. Rose pointed all this out to everyone in the pilothouse.

"Maybe the map was poorly drawn," Humphrey said.

"If Blackbeard made such precise calculations for latitude and longitude," Virginia said, "he would not have tolerated a poor drawing of the island itself."

"This here cove is the wrong shape, but there can't be two uncharted islands in the same place," Humphrey said.

"That pile looks like the aftermath of an avalanche," Rick said.

"And one that happened a long time ago going by the barnacles and shellfish up around the high tide line on those rocks," Damien said.

"The wind and sea whipped up by a hurricane may have scoured out the sand at the hill's base," Rick said, "and then it crashed down into the cove. That would have been something to see. And can you imagine the noise!"

The crew had all come up on deck. Damien ordered two of them forward to drop anchor. They did and the flukes hit bottom almost immediately.

"Damn," Damien said. "This is shallow as a bayou. Good thing my *bâteau* draws little water."

"Another reason this island may have remained unreported," Rose said. "With the avalanche filling so much of the cove, any ships that did come across the island would have found the cove unusable. No need to report a place no one could use as a safe harbor."

"Safe enough for our little shrimper, though." Damien shouted to a sailor on the bow. The sailor kicked the anchor rope and shouted something back. "The anchor is secure. Plenty more daylight. How's about we go ashore and find *beaucoup* pirate treasure?"

# CHAPTER TEN

Rose had to admit that Damien's idea of exploring the island was exciting. But the bunch of them had very little sleep last night, and the seasickness had taken its toll. With only a few hours of daylight left, the prudent move would be to sit tight, get a good meal in now that her stomach wasn't in turmoil, knock out a good night's sleep, and hit the island just after dawn. The treasure had been here for over two hundred years. It would still be here tomorrow. She was about to propose this plan when Rick cut in.

"Absolutely!" he said. "Let's go!"

"Rick," Rose said, "let's not rush in there half-assed."

"I'm fully assed, my dear wife. And," he cupped a hand to one ear, "I can hear the clink of Spanish pieces of eight coming from just off the beach. They're demanding we rescue them from this deserted island. This mission of mercy cannot be delayed."

Damien barked some orders to the men at the stern. They went below and returned with two deflated, yellow life rafts. One of the men also brought the end of an air hose up with him. They set the rafts on deck and began to inflate them. In no time, the two rafts were ready to go.

Damien went below and returned with two old rifles slung over his shoulders.

Virginia gasped. "What are those for? There's no one else here."

"That we know of, missy. But just because there's no people don't mean there's no dangers." He passed the rifles to two crewmen. "I've had too many unwelcome surprises in my line of work."

"Damien's dead-on," Humphrey said. "Ain't never regretted being over-armed in a situation."

Rose turned to whisper in Rick's ear. "I'm not thrilled about having this ragged-looking crew carrying guns."

"As long as Damien's in charge," Rick whispered, "I'm sure nothing will get out of hand."

One of the men dropped a rifle and it clattered on the deck.

"I'm pretty sure," he added.

The men slipped the two rafts overboard. It was decided to keep Humphrey on board to mind the ship since his ankle would keep him from hiking around the island. Damien passed down some gear into both rafts "just in case they got lucky" and then the rest of them piled in. Rose and Rick were in the same raft with two crewmen. Damien, Virginia, and three other crewmen were in the other raft. The group pushed off to the shore.

Rick leaned in to Rose. "I hope we can find that spot marked with the pentagon. In my mind this island was a lot smaller than it turned out to be. And over two hundred years all of this tropical growth could have overgrown any clues."

"From here on in," Rose said, "we rely on your legendary luck."

"Then we're as good as millionaires already."

The raft ran aground a few feet short of the beach and the two crewmen got out. Rick followed them over the side. The water was pleasantly warm, and clearer than anything he ever saw in the cloudy waters around Savannah.

Rose stood up and the crewmen waved her to sit back down. Then they began to try and heave the boat fully ashore.

"Oh, please," she said. "I can get my feet wet just like any man."

She jumped over the side and landed in calf-deep water. Rick laughed at the satisfied look on her face. One could treat Rose like a lady, but never like a little girl, and she reveled in showing men the distinction.

The four of them brought the raft up above the high tide line. The one without a rifle slung a large coil of rope over one shoulder and Rick did the same. Rose grabbed a shovel from the raft.

Damien's raft had fallen a bit behind the first and was just coming ashore. Suddenly, two pairs of dark-colored bumps six inches across and over a foot apart broke the surface midway between the raft and the boat. Eyelids rolled up on each to reveal slit-pupiled eyes so yellow they practically glowed. The eyes locked on Damien's raft as the unaware men popped over the side and pulled the raft ashore.

Rick's heart skipped a beat. Those looked like alligator eyes. He'd seen more than enough of them in the swampy areas outside the city. But the size and spacing were bizarre, at least twice as large and far apart as any gator he'd ever seen. Then a second set surfaced to the left of the first. This set seemed to be looking straight at him.

The bumps rose and the heads of two alligators surfaced. But they weren't like any alligator he'd seen before. Instead of broad, flat snouts, these had very narrow snouts with huge, sharp teeth jutting from both the top and the bottom. As the tails swept back and forth propelling them to the shore, Rick got an idea of the full length of the creatures, and they had to be almost forty feet long. That wasn't possible.

"Rick?" Rose said. "Do you see--?"

With a silent swish of its tail, the alligators closed on the four people standing near the second raft.

One of the two crewmen from Rick's raft unshouldered his rifle and took aim at the gators. He fired and water splashed in a spot right between the gator's eyes. The reptile didn't even flinch.

The gunshot alerted the others that there was some kind of danger. Their heads swiveled in all directions until they saw the two behemoths heading straight for them. Two crewmen, Virginia, and Damien scrambled up the beach for the trees.

Their crewman with a rifle stood his ground and brought it to bear on the nearest gator. He fired as fast as he could cycle the rifle's bolt. Three rounds seemed to hit their mark on. They made no difference. The beast kept coming.

The crewman from Rick's raft kept shooting as well. The gators focused on the second, closer raft, undeterred by the bullets or the noise. They hit the shore and then raced across the sand with an unholy burst of speed. The second raft's rifleman was so focused on firing, and confident that it would prove deadly, that he did not turn and run. One of the gators knocked him down.

Rick dropped his coil of rope and grabbed a shovel from the raft.

"Do you think that shovel is going to help?" Rose said.

"I don't think it's going to hurt. Beats being completely defenseless. Get off the beach."

Rose nodded and sprinted across the sand for the jungle.

Rick turned to see if the attacked crewman could be saved. It became immediately clear that he could not. The gator opened its jaws wide and clamped them shut on the man's head. It snapped free and the gator pulled away. The crewman's body pumped a fountain of blood from its severed neck and then went still.

The second gator saw it had lost its prey to its brother, and turned to Rick's half of the party. It charged over the other raft. Its mighty claws slashed through the rubber with several deep booms.

The remaining armed crewman seemed to realize he wasn't going to stop this thing with a rifle. He turned and bolted up the beach. Rick and the other crewman had the same idea. They charged into the jungle.

Rick crashed through the undergrowth. Sharp palms slashed at his arms and a carpet of vines threatened to tangle his feet. A few yards ahead, he could see Rose, eyes wide with panic waving him on. He prayed this wouldn't be the last image he had of her before he died.

Behind them, the gator made it just beyond the first few trees. Then vines snared its forelegs and it skidded to a halt. Its head slammed sideways into a tree. The gator blinked and went still, as if the impact had stunned it.

Rick made it to Rose. They embraced and he'd never been more grateful to feel her touch.

"Oh my God," she said. "That thing almost killed you."

"The alligator hasn't been born that can keep us apart," Rick said.

"Wasn't no gator," Damien said. The survivors from the other raft joined them in the jungle. "That was a caiman. Like a gator but *beaucoup* meaner. They live in the Caribbean."

"There are gators that big on all these islands?" Virginia said.

"Oh, no. Not big like that. Never seen anything big like that."

"Might be another reason Blackbeard liked this island," Rick said. "If he could figure out a way around those giant caimans, they would be excellent guards against any treasure hunters that might drop by."

"The map," Rose took out her copy and unfolded it. "One of the strange symbols in the harbor was this sideways V with lines sticking out of the inside of the V. All of a sudden that looks a lot like the open mouth of a caiman."

"A reminder from the mapmaker of danger in the cove?" Damien said.

"Even Blackbeard couldn't have gotten past those things," Rose said. "We barely got to shore when they attacked, and who knows how many are out there. Wild reptiles aren't much for being trained."

"You forget the witch," Virginia said. "The stories say that she could cast a spell to make the island itself defend Blackbeard's treasure."

"Virginia, there's no such thing as witches," Rick said. "And there aren't any magic powers out there to grow killer caimans."

"I don't know," Damien said. "Plenty of witchcraft practiced up in the bayou. Even the voodoo that came over with the slaves from Haiti. People put the *gris-gris* on things. Could be the same right here."

"Please," Rick said. "We were attacked by caimans. Damn big caimans, but still caimans. They just grow larger here. There's no witchcraft required to get a predator to hunt."

"And we need to get out of their hunting ground," Rose said.

"Louisiana gators don't like to be far from water," Damien said. "Pirate caimans are probably the same. Let's get up on high ground."

"The pentagon location indicated on the map should be just a short distance south of where we are," Rick said.

"Really?" Rose said. "After that you still want to look for treasure?"

"If we don't," Damien said, "what did my man die for?"

“We are too close to quit,” Virginia said. “We’ve come too far.”

The crewman with a rifle said something in Cajun.

“And Gustave says my men still need a payday,” Damien said.

“Consensus is we’re heading for the treasure,” Rick said.

“And how would we get it back to the boat?” Rose said.

“We’ll cross that bridge when we come to it.”

Given the condition of the rafts though, it seemed like some of those bridges were already burned.

# CHAPTER ELEVEN

From across the cove came the toot of the shrimp boat's horn.

"Sounds like old Humphrey's worried about us," Rick said.

"I'll go back and signal him," Damien said.

"I'll go with you." Rick gave his shovel to Rose. "The rest of you should stay here, as far from the caimans as you can."

Damien turned to Gustave. "You stay alert."

Gustave was wide-eyed and so twitchy he made the rifle bounce in his hands. There was no chance this guy was going to relax. He was more likely to have a heart attack.

Rick and Damien made a cautious journey back through the jungle. Save for the chirp and buzz of insects, there weren't any sounds. That put Rick a bit more at ease. There was no way a giant caiman could crawl through this place without making a lot of noise.

They got back to the beach, about fifty yards from where they'd come ashore. Both rafts lay shredded and deflated on the sand. The crewman's corpse was gone, but a big red blood stain coated the ground where he'd been killed. A jumble of caiman footprints marred the sand around the water's edge. It seemed the beach was safe, at least for now.

"Well, we don't have a way back to the boat now," Rick said. "We're going to need to find something on this island that floats."

Out in the cove, Humphrey had raised the anchor and fired up the engine. Now the shrimper idled about sixty feet from shore. Rick could see Humphrey framed by the pilothouse window, scanning the shore with a pair of binoculars. Rick stepped out from the trees and waved. The horn on the boat tooted again. Damien stepped beside him as Humphrey piloted the boat closer to the shore.

"Don't you run my boat aground!" Damien shouted.

Humphrey slowed the boat to a stop and hobbled out onto the bow.

"I saw what happened on the beach," Humphrey said. "Is everyone else okay?"

"We're all fine," Rick said. "Safety tip for you: Do not go swimming."

"Didn't bring my trunks no-how. You think those things gonna attack the boat?"

"Nah," Rick said. "Never seen a gator attack anything bigger than itself, and those caimans are big, but not that big."

"Humphrey, you just hold on out there," Damien said. "The rafts are shot so since we can't get back to you, we're going to scout out the location marked on the map. Maybe we'll find something that we can use to get back out to you."

"We may also find pirate treasure," Rick said.

"Here's hoping y'all do both," Humphrey said. "I'll be anchored here and waiting on y'all to come back."

Humphrey went back to the pilothouse. The old shrimper backed away from the shore. Then the anchor line unspooled from the forward winch and dropped the anchor into the water.

"That's no way to drop an anchor," Damien lamented. "See what happens when a flyboy tries to do a sailor's job?"

The two of them salvaged what gear they could from the rafts. They returned to the group and updated them on Humphrey, the boat, and the deflated rafts. The bad news was met with silence.

"Gustave, take the lead with the rifle," Damien said as he threw a coil of rope over his shoulder. "Angelo, Carlito, Hugo, you grab this gear for when we find the treasure."

The three stepped up and grabbed what they could. Rick shouldered a coil of rope. Virginia and Rose stuffed flashlights in their pockets and picked up a shovel each. Then everyone began to hike south.

The island's dense jungle made them pay for every step. The sharpened edges of palm branches drew blood at even a passing touch. Vines and dense undergrowth snagged their feet. The sparse, taller trees only offered short respites from the tropical sun.

"This jungle is the worst," Rose said.

"No, it's the best news ever," Rick said. "By being so overgrown, it means that other people haven't been here for a long time, maybe since Blackbeard's last visit."

"You love to give the worst circumstances a positive spin, don't you?"

"I used that reasoning to convince you to marry me. I'm sticking to a winning formula."

"The jury is still out on whether I consider that a win."

At the head of the column, Gustave gave a shout and pointed just off to the left. The peaked side of a stone building stuck out of the jungle.

"We have a winner!" Rick said. "Give that man a cigar."

The group angled to approach the structure. Once they got close to it, they broke out into a higher, sandy patch of ground. In the center stood the remains of a five-sided building. Rick's first thought was that it was about the size of the one-room schoolhouse he'd attended as a child. The building had once hosted a peaked roof, but time and the elements had destroyed that long ago. The windows no longer had any glass, if they ever had any to begin with, and the front door was missing. The textured block walls contained a multitude of white, tan, and brown hues.

"It doesn't look like a bank vault," Rick said. "But here's hoping Blackbeard used it as one."

Damien had his men keep an eye on things outside the building as he, Rose, Rick, and Virginia went inside.

Rick had nurtured a hope that there would be a pile of treasure in the center of the building, waiting to be carted off to new owners. He was disappointed. The building stood empty, the roof wide open to the sky. The floor had been made from felled palm tree trunks. As they stepped on them, the wood crumbled into small bits.

Rose examined the block walls in detail. "These are made of coquina. It's a naturally occurring limestone embedded with seashells and marine life. It's common all around the Caribbean. The Spanish built early forts in the Americas out of this."

"You think the Spanish built this?" Rick said.

"No, or the island would have been on their maps. Whoever did build it knew about coquina, and why it was the stuff to use. It practically absorbs cannon balls without breaking. If someone was going to build a place to make a last stand in case of attack, it would look just like this."

"And the trees around this building are older and taller than the rest," Damien said. "This high point has stayed dry during the worst hurricanes."

"Then the treasure's got to be buried right here," Rick said.

"Under these big logs?" Damien said. "Pretty hard to move. Blackbeard could never come back alone to make a withdrawal."

Rose stood before a section of the wall and swept away some accumulated sand and debris. She exposed a map carved into the coquina.

"This is a duplicate of the parchment map," she said. "Even the same size. I'll bet the pencil drawing of the map was copied straight from this one, maybe even traced. Blackbeard definitely built this place."

On the other side of the room, Virginia blew some sand from a wall and exposed a symbol about two feet across. It looked like a diamond with two wavy lines running through it. She traced a finger over the lines as if she was drawing them.

"What's that?" Rick said.

"A witchcraft symbol." Her voice had an eerie, dreamy quality to it.

"Like there is some *gris-gris* on this place?" Damien said.

"No, not like that. This is a sign of welcome, an indicator that the building, perhaps the island, supports spells from the dark arts. It would be part of a cleansing spell that would make any following spells even stronger."

"Proof that Blackbeard and witches have been here," Rick said. "We're definitely in the right place."

"But not the right place for treasure, I think," Damien said. "Not under these logs in here. And not out there among the roots of all those trees. That would have been *beaucoup* days of digging for a dozen men."

"Then why mark this place on the map at all?"

Rose had been walking the perimeter of the room, sweeping carvings on the walls clean. "This isn't a treasury. It's a chart room."

All around them she'd uncovered locations and numbers carved into the wall. Each also had an arrow pointing in a specific direction. Other, broader, wavy arrows contained numbers and dates.

"These names?" she said. "These are locations, followed by distance and bearings. The wavy lines are currents, with speeds and the dates they run hard. This was Blackbeard's command center. Orient a chart on a table in the center of the room, and from here he could plan where to attack and how to best make his escape."

"And the pentagon building design works better for that than a rectangle," Rick said. "And is much more defensible if Blackbeard had to make a last stand here."

"But that still leaves the rest of the island to search to find where he stashed his loot," Damien said.

Rose went over to the eastern wall. She brushed some more dirt from where a solitary arrow sat alone. Beneath it was a single number. "This is the only arrow in here with only one number attached to it, a distance with no compass bearing or time notation. Could be paces, could be feet, could be yards."

Rose stepped over to a nearby window and looked out along the direction the arrow pointed. "And the arrow points to the extinct volcano."

# CHAPTER TWELVE

"So there's treasure buried on the mountain?" Damien said.

"Or the clue to finding it is on the mountain," Rose said. "One way or another, this arrow is telling us to go in that direction."

Rick looked out the window at the setting sun. "Whatever is up there, we aren't going to find it today. Soon we'll be stumbling around in the dark. This is as good a place as any to hole up for the night."

Damien gave the walls a once over. "Better than sleeping in the open."

"My husband always finds me first-class accommodations," Rose said.

"It's my special talent," Rick said.

"Flying would be a more welcome special talent right now," Rose said, "and then you could get us back to the boat."

Damien went to the doorway and called in his four men. He gave them a briefing in Cajun. When he was finished, the men dropped all their supplies and tools in the center of the room, and then Gustave and Hugo took the rifle and went back outside.

"Those two are on guard duty," Damien said. "Carlito and Angelo will rotate with them every four hours."

"You said caimans wouldn't come this far from the water," Rose said.

"I also said caimans were only a few feet long," Damien said. "I'd hate to be unprepared if I turned out to be wrong again."

Rick began an inventory of the gear they'd gotten from the rafts before the attack. There were several coils of rope, a half dozen flashlights, shovels, and the rifle Damien's men had. He stepped back and smiled. "We could be worse off."

"How?" Rose said. "We're trapped on an island with giant killer caimans and no food or water. How much worse could this get?"

Rick thought it was a win that they likely still had what they needed to move the treasure once they found it. But he wasn't about to volunteer that to try and improve Rose's disposition. Her initially tepid enthusiasm for the treasure hunt had turned ice-cold. He hoped she'd feel better after a good night's sleep.

"We'll solve those problems tomorrow," he said. "Now, I'll get a fire started. It'll get cool tonight, and nothing keeps wild animals away like open flames. They might not fear people, but they fear fire."

Rick went out into the jungle and collected an armful of dead branches and browned palm leaves. By the time he'd returned to the building, Damien had dug a firepit near the building's center. Rick arranged the firewood in and beside the pit. He patted his pockets.

"I could use a match."

Virginia sat against the side wall. She lit herself a cigarette, then tossed the box of matches to Rick. "Light it up."

By the time darkness completely fell, Rick had a good-sized fire going in the old chart house. He and Rose sat in one corner, opposite Virginia. Rick had an arm around Rose and her head rested on his shoulder. Damien's first set of men had been replaced by the others, and Damien was engaged in a low conversation with them near the building's doorway as he rolled himself a cigarette.

"How much do you trust Damien?" Rose said.

"Humphrey brought him in on the deal," Rick said. "So I trust him."

"Humphrey's circle of accomplices is usually bound together by shared greed, more than shared good morals. What if instead of being trustworthy, Damien was simply available?"

"I think you're being paranoid."

"Blackbeard left half his crew on this island after hiding his treasure," Rose said. "What's to keep Damien from leaving us here the same way?"

"Maybe because he isn't a pirate?"

"He's a smuggler. That's pretty close in my book."

"I'm more worried about Virginia," Rick said. "She knows a lot more about all this witchcraft lore than I'd expected."

"And it's a good thing she does. All the research I did was on pirates and the general time period. She's been a big help so far. She confirmed what those witch symbols on the walls meant. We'd have never known that."

"Witchcraft talk gives me, and most people, the willies," Rick said. "She's way too comfortable with it, excited even."

"Now you're being paranoid," Rose said. "You don't understand how researchers think about these things. We look at all of history clinically, detached. If every horrible thing I read about scared me, I couldn't read about anything. So she's matter-of-fact about all this witch stuff, and maybe a little excited about discovering what she's been researching for so long. It's no big deal."

"Well, I'm keeping a close eye on her for the rest of this trip."

"Yes," Rose said. "Watch for her to put on a big pointed black hat and ride around on a broom. Meanwhile, I'll keep an eye on Damien, the self-professed criminal."

"Let's hope that we get home safe and sound and all of our suspicions were for nothing."

A few hours later, a shout awakened Rick. He and Rose had fallen asleep leaning on each other and as he jolted awake, so did she. He wondered if he'd only dreamed the noise until a gunshot rang out in the night.

"Stick close," he said to Rose. He jumped up and turned on his flashlight. Across the room, Damien's flashlight lit up, followed by Virginia's. The four of them met at the doorway.

"Angelo!" Damien called out. He shined his light around the area outside the building and it found nothing.

A flashlight came bobbing across the clearing from the right. Carlito appeared, carrying the rifle. He looked panicked. He and Damien exchanged some rapid-fire Cajun.

Damien turned back to the others. "Carlito said something came out of the darkness. Something big. Angelo screamed. When Carlito ran to where he had been sitting, Angelo was gone."

"Was it a caiman?" Virginia said.

Carlito said something to Damien.

"He said he could not tell what it was," Damien translated.

Damien took the rifle from Carlito and told him to stay at the door. "Gustave and I are going for Angelo."

"I'm with you." Rick grabbed a shovel, more for defense than offense, and followed the two men into the darkness.

Only the buzz of insect life sounded in the night. Rick imagined that every step each of them took in the sand sounded like a crash, calling creatures in the night to their next victims.

"He was on guard right over here," Damien said.

The three played their flashlights across the ground as they approached the southwest corner of the clearing. When they made it to the trees, the ground went from flat to churned. Broken branches and trampled plants testified that something big had been here.

Damien's flashlight stopped playing back and forth and lit up one place on the ground. A puddle of wet blood had pooled inside a footprint in the sand.

Rick went to examine the plants. Something shiny lay beneath a broken tree branch. He plucked it up and examined it. It was a green-tinted scale that looked like reptile skin. The texture was completely different from a caiman's skin.

He showed it to Damien. "If there's something big enough to shed this scale, we shouldn't be trying to find it in the dark."

Damien rubbed the scale between his fingers. "You're right," Damien said. "I don't like the looks of this. We'd better pull back to the building and stoke the fire. Whatever's out here, we'll see it if it comes back and get a clearer shot at it in the firelight."

"And Angelo?"

Damien stood up and started back for the building. "He's probably hiding, or passed out. He can take care of himself."

The three returned to the building where the nervous guard at the door had a shovel in his hand and looked ready to clobber anything that moved, including them. Rose had stoked the fire and gotten a bright blaze going.

"Any signs of Angelo out there?" Rose said.

"No good ones," Rick said. "Something attacked him and dragged him off."

"Something?"

"I don't know what it was, but I can tell you what it wasn't." Rick handed Rose the reptile scale. "It wasn't a caiman."

# CHAPTER THIRTEEN

Knowing that a second kind of deadly creature stalked the island, no one seemed to get much sleep. Rose knew that she didn't. She spent the night tending the fire, adding fuel when the flames stopped lighting up the interior of the building.

At one point, Rick dozed off leaning against the corner. Rose went to a window by the doorway. Gustave stood just outside with his rifle pointing in the general direction of the jungle. The jungle's shadowy outline hung like a curtain at the clearing's edge.

She wondered how Rick had talked her into this in the first place, and in a broader sense, how he managed to do it so often. The man had a knack for making the impossible seem simple to accomplish, the rewards to far outweigh the risks he casually brushed off.

Rick stepped up beside her. "Two-to-one says you are about to call room service to bring up champagne."

"You were sound asleep seconds ago."

"I guess not having you there woke me up."

Rose looked back out the window. "I can't believe you got me into this, trapped on an uncharted island with a crew of smugglers, facing at least two kinds of giant monsters."

"And to think your father didn't want you to marry me."

"Be serious. I'm not the person to be in situations like this. I'm an antiques dealer, a researcher, a reader." She turned and grabbed the front of his shirt. "You promise me we're going to get out of this alive."

"Rosie, we're going to get out of this *because* you're here. You'll have the brains to get us to the treasure. I'm just the muscle to help haul it home. And Damien's men will keep all the bad monsters away while we do it. Have I ever steered you wrong before?"

"Let me get a pen and paper to make a list."

"Don't worry. We'll manage this. Tomorrow morning, things will look better. We'll get a reasonable explanation for what happened to Angelo, we'll head up the mountain, and come down with treasure."

"It's just that simple?"

"It always is."

Actually, Rose's experiences were that Rick's plans were never that simple, but as usual, somehow Rick made it seem that this just might be the time things went smoothly.

#

Rick hadn't slept at all after Damien's crewman had been dragged away. He had been afraid to drift off, certain that doing so would be an invitation for the creature to return and make Rose its next victim. Rick sat with his back against the wall, facing the doorway with a shovel at his side.

He'd feigned sleep in the hope that if he seemed relaxed, Rose would relax as well, but that plan had taken a while to work. His wife had finally fallen asleep with her head on his lap. Rick's leg had fallen asleep right after Rose had. She'd twitched and mumbled several times in her sleep, and each time he held her tight, as if he could squeeze the nightmares from her slumber, and each time she'd calmed down.

Dawn's arrival was a welcome sight. While sunrise might not keep away whatever creature was out there, at least they'd have a better chance of fighting it off if they could see it.

Rose's eyelids flickered open. She squinted against the daylight.

"Rise and shine," Rick said. "We have a full day of fun scheduled for you here at Blackbeard's Resort."

As if her brain had finally woken enough to process their dire situation, she sat straight up. "What did I miss?"

"Nothing." Rick gave his numb leg a shake and started to massage some circulation back into it. "No one saw anything all night."

"Did you get any sleep?"

"As far as you know, yes." Rick stood and steadied himself against the wall as pins and needles wracked his right leg. "Now that it's light, I'm going to check the scene of the attack again. Order us breakfast while I'm out, will you? Something light. I don't want to feel bloated."

"Don't get killed out there."

"That's on the top of my to-do list."

Rick made his way to where Damien stood just outside the doorway. Virginia sat alone against a far wall, smoking a cigarette. One of the strange witch's symbols was right over her head. Her eyes were closed and her lips were moving, as if she was speaking to herself, or praying. Rick didn't like the idea of her doing either.

At Damien's feet, Carlito sat outside the wall with the rifle in his lap. His bleary eyes said he also hadn't slept last night.

"Any signs of our predator out there?" Rick said.

"My men said it was quiet all night," Damien said. "I was about to take a look-see at where Angelo was attacked."

"My thoughts exactly."

Damien took the rifle from Carlito and Rick followed him back out to the jungle. Insects buzzed like the noise of a far-off crowd. The jungle seemed so different in the daylight, so bright and lively, so benign. It was as if the island had put on a smiling mask to hide the murderous tendencies it had displayed so far.

They arrived at the location they'd inspected in the dark last night. It looked much worse in the daylight. In addition to the dried blood on the ground, blood also splattered the leaves around the area. Shreds of cloth from Angelo's shirt and pants stuck out half-buried in the churned-up sand.

"Looky here," Damien said.

Beside him in the sand was a distinct, two-foot-wide footprint. The broad spacing of the long toes looked reptilian, but it was clearly different from the prints left by the caimans. The sharp impression of a large claw tipped the outline of each toe.

"Never seen prints like that," Damien said.

"Neither have I. Whatever it is, it's damn big. The tracks point south, and the snapped leaf stalks say that's the way this thing carried Angelo off."

Damien turned around to head back to the building.

"You don't want to look for him?" Rick said.

"You mean look for his body. No. He's dead, we're alive. Let's keep it that way and head up the mountain."

While that was an eminently practical way to look at it, it did seem heartless. "Are you sure?"

"You'd be surprised to find out how many men I lose in my line of work."

Rick figured that was likely true. But he doubted Damien had lost many to giant monsters before.

Rose felt sorry for Virginia. Rose had Rick by her side, but Virginia was alone, surrounded by strange men on a hostile island. She doubted that the woman had gotten any sleep last night. Rose went over to her. Virginia sat against a wall, just finishing a cigarette. She pressed the butt into the sand and rubbed it out. As Rose got closer, Virginia smoothed the sand in front of her with the sole of her foot.

"Sleep okay?" Rose said.

"Not bad, all things considered."

Rose noticed Virginia did look much more rested than Rose felt. If the woman had managed to catch some sleep, good for her.

"This is a little more dangerous than I'd imagined it would be," Rose said. "Sorry to get you into it."

"I got myself into it. I volunteered, remember? I didn't expect that we'd find chests of pirate gold waiting for us on the beach."

"But you can't have expected giant monsters, either."

Virginia smiled. "Witchcraft protects the island. I did not expect it to give up its treasure, or mysteries, without a fight."

Rose had to give the woman credit for being so calm in the face of everything that had happened so far. Maybe the advertising in the magazines was right and smoking calmed the nerves.

"You sound like a true believer in all that witchcraft and magic stuff." Rose almost said *nonsense* instead of *stuff* and caught herself at the last second.

Virginia's eyes narrowed. "From as far back as man has records, reports of witchcraft are in them. Do you think a practice like that can persist so long without there being truth to it?"

"I don't know. Rick and I have certainly seen some strange things. But witchcraft seems to have gone out of style since the trials in Salem."

"What you call out of style may actually just be taken underground."

Before Rose could further explore Virginia's fascination with the history of these occult practices, Rick and Damien came back into the building. They did not have Angelo with them. That could only mean that the man was dead. Damien barked a Cajun command. Gustave, Carlito and Hugo gathered around him. Rick went over to Rose.

"The attack location looks worse in the daylight," Rick said. "And there are big footprints unlike anything I've ever seen."

"Nothing as simple and explainable as a jaguar?"

"Or as small. Damien and I agreed the best bet is to keep heading up the mountain, hopefully out of this thing's hunting range."

"He still wants to go on after having two crewmen die?" Rose said.

"He's adamant."

Rose's stomach growled and she rolled her eyes. "I wish we'd brought some food with us."

"I'm more concerned with water. Dehydration will knock us down before starvation will."

The group came together at the doorway. Damien distributed the gear among everyone, with Rick and himself saddled with coils of rope. He handed Virginia and Rose the digging tools.

Damien gave Gustave an order in Cajun. The man grimaced, unshouldered his rifle, and took the lead. He did not look very excited about getting to be first. Carlito followed Gustave, and Hugo took up the rear position behind everyone else.

As they made their way through the jungle, Rick was on high alert, waiting for something to charge from among the trees. The rest of the group didn't seem any more relaxed. The tension among them all was almost palpable.

Damien kept checking a compass and giving Gustave directions to angle a little right or a little left. As they crossed the island in the direction the supposed treasure arrow had indicated, the ground got steeper. Sweat broke out on Rick's brow and his breathing became labored.

At one particularly precipitous section, Rose slipped and Rick caught her before she could fall. She kicked away the loose soil beneath her feet to expose glossy, black rock. She knelt down and ran her fingers across it.

"This is solid basalt," she said. "We aren't climbing a mountain. This is a volcano."

"Volcano?" Damien said.

"Extinct volcano," Rose added. "Thousands of years extinct from the looks of it. But that's how this island was born. At one point a pocket of collapsing magma probably created the cove we sailed into."

"So, while there may be giant creatures after us," Rick said, "on the bright side, the island itself isn't trying to kill us."

"Yet," Damien added.

# CHAPTER FOURTEEN

A few minutes later, they came across a stream. Clear water cascaded down over glassy black rocks that the stream had scoured clean.

The group stopped. Rick knelt down and scooped up a handful of water. He sniffed it and it didn't smell bad. He touched his lips to it. He winced. "It's fresh water, but it's got a tang to it. But if I'm picking between an upset stomach or dehydration, the upset stomach wins."

"I'm glad dehydration won't kill us," Damien said.

"Wouldn't want to cheat the caimans out of their chance to do it," Rick said.

Everyone knelt by the water, cupped handfuls from the stream, and drank. Rick drank until his stomach bulged, hoping that would offset his growing hunger pangs.

Below them, the stream curved off to the left and headed for the aftermath of the landslide that had halved the cove. Above them, the stream ran down from the same direction they'd been heading. The plants along both sides of the stream had been beaten back or crushed into struggling nubs.

Damien pointed upstream. "This would be *beaucoup* easier route up the mountain."

"That might be because animals like the one from last night have been crushing all the plants," Rose said.

"Could be." Damien ordered Carlito to take the rifle and the lead and follow the stream uphill.

After a while, they found the stream's source. A broad pond stretched out in a level clearing. The far side of the pond was a solid cliff of weathered basalt. A row of mottled gray and green boulders ringed the pond's edge at the base of the cliff. Tall palms along the pond's seaward edge swayed in the onshore breeze.

"I can't believe there's a spring coming out of an extinct island volcano," Rose said.

"I'll bet it isn't," Rick said. "I'll bet rainwater and condensation off that cliff keep this little pond topped off."

"Another reason this island made a good hideaway for Blackbeard," Virginia said. "A source to refill the fresh water stores on his ships."

"They weren't about to drag barrels up and down this mountain to get water. The landslide must have buried the spot where the stream enters the cove."

"Which means the water under that landslide used to be pretty deep," Damien said.

"This pond is beautiful," Rose said. "Maybe if the pirates had come up here more often, they'd have been inspired to do less pirating."

A rumble sounded from the far end of the pond. Rick's heart raced and he scanned the face of the cliff. There weren't any tumbling rocks, but something had made that sound. Rick stepped over so he was back-to-back with Rose.

"You heard that?" Rick said.

"I couldn't miss it," Rose said. "Did you see what made it?"

"No, and I'm hoping none of us ever do."

Plants down the side of the pond behind them swayed and snapped. Whatever had bellowed across the water wasn't the only creature around them.

At the far western end of the pond, one of the boulders moved. As it rose, it became clear that this was not a boulder, though the camouflage shading of its skin had matched the cliff face behind it to perfection. It was a giant iguana, about twenty feet long, and its powerful tail accounted for half that length. Sun glinted off its scaly body. Unlike the caimans, this creature's legs raised it several feet off the ground. It looked like it could run down prey faster than the caimans had.

This enormous iguana was practically as large as the caimans they'd escaped, easily fifteen feet long and several feet wide. Its huge head and jaws looked large enough to swallow a person in one bite.

Rose had seen it as well. She reached down and grabbed Rick's hand. "Do you think it's seen us?"

Its black eyes narrowed as it locked on the humans on the beach.

"It has now," Rick said.

Then the situation got worse. A second iguana crashed out of the forest where all the commotion had been behind them. At ten yards away, the size of the creature was terrifying. A crest of spiky plumes ran down its elongated head and partway to its back. What looked like large circular shields protruded from its face beneath its black eyes. It hissed at the group. The creature stank of musk and decay.

The first iguana sprinted up the shore toward the group. They were trapped.

Rick knew turning and running would be suicide. These things would be on them in seconds. He dropped his coil of rope and gripped the shovel Rose held. "May I?"

"Be my guest."

Rick grabbed the shovel and held it across his chest. He wasn't sure what the hell he was going to do with this to keep them safe, but it was better than using his bare hands.

The closest iguana charged Hugo. He sprinted to the side, but the creature whipped its tail in his direction. The tail hit him and sent him across the sand like a skipping stone.

Gustave wasn't waiting to play defense. He aimed the rifle at the iguana that had just sidelined Hugo and fired. The rifle barked and Gustave instantly cycled another bullet into the chamber. The iguana's head jerked back as its left eye exploded in a spray of blood and fluid.

Now half-blinded, the iguana whipped its head back and forth as if trying to locate this strange threat. The creature stopped with its good eye fixed on the crewman who'd blinded it.

Gustave did not flinch. The rifle had never left his shoulder, his aim had never wavered from the iguana's head. He squeezed the trigger again. The second round found its mark, the iguana's remaining eye. It burst and the iguana reeled sideways back into the jungle. It thrashed in the undergrowth, likely half from pain and half from the inconceivable event of its world going dark.

Gustave cycled the bolt and the ejecting shell jammed in the breech. He took a knee and tried to yank the bolt free.

The second iguana charged up through the sand, heading for the rest of the group.

Carlito raised his shovel over one shoulder like a baseball bat. The iguana attacked him first, pounding across the ground with its jaws wide. Its claws sent clods of dirt and grass flying behind it.

Damien had bragged about the bravery of his crew, and Carlito lived up to the hype. The iguana closed on him and he stood his ground. At the last minute he dodged to the side and delivered a massive blow to the iguana's head.

The iguana didn't flinch. Instead, it whipped its head against Carlito and knocked him flat on the ground. The shovel skidded across the sand. The iguana hissed and the semi-conscious crewman moaned.

The iguana chomped down on Carlito's chest. His body folded and blood spurted in all directions. His scream went silent. The iguana lifted its head and the limp corpse sagged in the creature's jaws like a frown.

Damien screamed a series of curses in Cajun and ran for the fallen shovel.

The iguana in the jungle stopped flailing. It raised its nose in the air and sniffed. Blood coated the sides of its head. It turned toward Rick and Rose, cocked its head, and hissed.

"Rick, it smells us!" Rose said.

The iguana sprinted out of the jungle and straight for the two of them.

Rick thought fast. "Get down!"

Rose knelt beside Rick. He angled the shovel at the charging reptile.

The iguana closed on him fast. He lifted the shovel and held it shoulder-high like a harpooner, with his left hand supporting the shaft behind the spade and his right hand wrapped around the top of the handle. His heart pounded so hard that he could feel his pulse thrum against the wood.

The iguana opened its jaws and hissed a blast of fetid breath over Rick. With its maw only a foot away, Rick let the shovel fly. He thrust it into the iguana's mouth and up. The sharp end of the spade pierced the iguana's upper pallet. Blood splashed everywhere and the iguana's momentum drove the shovel in deep. Rick let go as the iguana's jaw slammed shut. The tip of the handle stuck out between its teeth.

The iguana roared and backed away. It scratched at the handle with one foot, but could not get a grip on the thin, slick shaft. It wailed and tried in vain to shake the shovel free as it retreated.

Damien had less success with the other iguana. He struck the creature on the snout with the shovel like a man trying to get a dog to drop something. The iguana wasn't cowed. It spit the crewman's corpse on the ground and butted Damien head on. Damien flew backward and landed on the ground spread eagle. The iguana charged and slapped a foot on Damien's chest.

Just as it seemed Damien was doomed, the iguana paused. The other iguana flailing on the beach did as well. Both cocked their heads as if they heard something interesting. Then the iguanas retreated, both diving into the jungle and disappearing.

Rick exhaled in relief. Damien sat up and rubbed his chest. Rose stood up and grabbed Rick's arm to help him up.

"That was close," she said.

"Too close," Rick said. "I'd played my last card."

Damien got to his feet. Rick realized he couldn't see Virginia. He turned to see her kneeling by some trees at the clearing's edge. She ran her hands across the sand in front of her, stood up, and ran over to Rose.

"Are you two okay?" she said.

"Yes," Rose said. "But not by much."

Damien walked by the crewman's corpse. He shook his head and continued over to the others. Gustave helped a limping Hugo to join them as well.

"Two deadly giant creatures defending the island so far," Virginia said. "Do any of you still doubt the power of a witch's curse now?"

Rick was on his way to becoming a believer.

# CHAPTER FIFTEEN

Rose didn't like the idea of fighting witchcraft. Mostly because she didn't know of any way to fight it, especially when it had giant monsters on its side.

Damien turned to Gustave. "Give me that rifle."

Gustave handed it to him. Damien tried to work the bolt and got nowhere. "*Couillon!* What have I told you about keeping these guns oiled? Look at the rust here."

Damien delivered a huge wad of spit into the breach. He worked it in with his stubby fingers. The process turned Rose's stomach. Then he picked up a big rock from the ground and smacked the handle on the bolt. On a second try, the bolt came free and the spent shell casing sailed off into the air. He handed the rifle back to Gustave. "Find something to grease that or it will jam again next time you shoot."

Gustave nodded and continued to work some of the rust off his rifle.

"I don't know what made those iguanas break off their attack," Rick said, "but I'd lay odds that they'll come back. I say we get moving up the mountain."

The group headed uphill with Rick in the lead this time and Rose right behind him.

"Rick?" Rose said. "What do you think about what Virginia said, about the witch's spell?"

"I don't know. I've always thought witchcraft was nonsense. Have we seen strange animals here? Sure we have. But this is an unexplored island. There are bound to be strange animals here. I've seen pictures of bizarre things from Australia, and that's an island."

She was going to correct him that it was a continent, but this wasn't the time for that. "Virginia is right.

History is filled with tales of witches and spells they cast. Even the Bible is. It can't be that none of those stories are true."

"We'll sort the explanations out later. All that matters now is that we stay alive. And that's about to get much easier. Once we get up out of this jungle, the odds turn in our favor. The rest of the hike up is across bare rock. Nowhere for any nasty animals to hide."

"We still have to go back through the jungle with the treasure if we find it, and somehow get back to the boat."

"We'll play that hand when it gets dealt. First, we get to the top of this mountain, interpret the clue the arrow was pointing us to, and then we'll conquer the next obstacle."

Rick had a penchant for making long odds sound short and difficult tasks easy. Rose was never quite sure if he really believed his rosy-outlook statements, was saying them for her benefit, or was maybe trying to convince himself.

Soon they came to the edge of the jungle. The ground abruptly changed from soil and flora to glazed, black stone. A few hardy pioneer plants poked up from the slag here and there, but for the most part it was barren as the moon. The group stepped out onto the rock and into the full force of the tropical sun.

"This proves the island was volcanic," Rose said. "This is lava from the last eruption. The flow made it this far down the mountain before it cooled."

"Before or after Blackbeard was here?" Damien said. "I'd hate to find out that the eruption covered up his treasure."

"I would say long before," Virginia said. "An eruption like this would have had a smoke plume visible for miles and miles. This island wouldn't have remained undiscovered."

Rose shook her head. There were still hundreds of feet of elevation to conquer, and while the slope was manageable, it was still plenty steep.

Damien swapped Hugo to the head of the column with the rifle and ordered him to keep climbing. Rose took a deep breath and followed Rick as he fell in behind Hugo.

A little while later she realized that the blazing sun was only going to be half the heat battle. The black rock beneath her feet absorbed the rays and sent tangible waves of radiated heat back up at her. Mental images of broiled fish came to mind and she pushed them away as quickly as she could.

After a lengthy hike, they finally closed on the old volcano's rim. Rick led them around it until they were centered on the cove below. From here it was easy to confirm that the theory of an avalanche was correct. Down at where the tree line would have been, the natural curve of the volcano had been flattened on this side. Out in the water, the old shrimp boat bobbed in the swell.

"I see Humphrey has not sunk my *cher bâteau* yet," Damien said. "What a relief."

Rose thought Damien's concern for his boat was a lot stronger than for the crewmen who'd died on this trip.

From here they could also get a pretty good overview of the island. It was about two miles across and shaped just like the outline on the map. Tropical forest ringed the barren volcano top like a monk's haircut. Nothing stood out as different or gave any indication of being an optimal place to hide the treasure of a lifetime.

Rose turned to Virginia who was standing behind her. "Well, where would Blackbeard hide his treasure, if he was even here at all?"

"Oh, he was here," Virginia said.

She pointed down at her feet. Etched into the stone was the skeleton and arrow sign of Blackbeard the pirate. Beneath that was the date 1717, and an arrow that pointed to the cove.

"Come see!" Hugo said from inside the crater rim behind them.

The group clambered up the slope to the edge. On the other side, the circular volcano crater stretched across about a hundred feet. The slopes were covered with small pumice stones that looked like black sponges packed in dark sand. Hugo stood just inside the crater rim with the rifle slung over his shoulder.

About twenty feet down, the crater bottom was completely different. It looked like a sheet of solid, obsidian glass. Several large boulders dotted the surface where the crumbled rim had sent them rolling down.

"That looks like the world's dirtiest ice rink," Rick said.

"The magma in the volcano cooled and left that surface," Rose said. "Sheltered from the wind, it was like a molten mineral pond."

"You sure know a lot about volcanoes," Rick said.

"I actually read the National Geographic magazines in the shop. You should give it a try."

"Seriously, if you can master the articles so well, there's really no point in *both* of us reading them, is there?"

"Uh, oh," Hugo said as the rock under his feet crumbled. He toppled over and began to skid downhill.

"*Mon Dieu!* Hugo!" Damien cried out.

Hugo grabbed for purchase, screamed, and recoiled as the sharp volcanic rock cut at his hands. Loosened rock began a small landslide in his wake. He rolled downhill faster, leaving a cloud of black dust. When he hit the dried lava field, he skidded out several yards across the slick surface before he came to a stop, surrounded by a spray of pumice stones.

Hugo sat up and shook his head. He looked up at the group, shrugged and laughed.

Suddenly the ground beneath him cracked in multiple directions, like thin spring ice on a lake. His laughter died and panic filled his face. Then all at once, the lava field beneath him collapsed and Hugo disappeared into the abyss it exposed. His echoed scream seemed to last forever, and then went silent.

# CHAPTER SIXTEEN

Damien headed for the gaping hole in the extinct volcano's floor. Rick grabbed him and held him back.

"You rush down there and you'll fall in there just like he did. Hold on."

Rick dropped the rope from his shoulder and took the other rope from Damien's. He knotted the two coils together and handed Damien the free end of one.

"Tie yourself off with this," Rick said. "We'll be your safety line if more of the crater collapses."

Damien wrapped the rope around his waist and tied a knot. He gave the crater a closer look, then began a slow descent down the slope. The stony surface shifted under his feet, but did not collapse. Rick, Gustave, Virginia, and Rose all held onto the rope and fed it to Damien as he sidestepped his way down the crater. He paused at the bottom by the glassy surface.

"He shouldn't go out there," Gustave said. "Hugo already broke through that."

Rick wasn't worried. "Look at that boulder just short of the hole. The surface hasn't cracked under that weight."

"If it's a pumice boulder," Rose said, "it might only weigh a few pounds."

Now Rick started to worry.

Damien edged forward in an awkward shuffle, left foot first, then his right foot up beside it. Soon he made it to the boulder. He rested against it for a moment. Then Damien gave the group at the crater rim a thumbs-up, and began to crawl to the edge of the hole.

Sweat began to form on Rick's palms. He worried he'd overpromised what the four of them could do if more of the pit's edge opened up while Damien was on it.

Damien made it to the jagged edge of the opening. He peered over, then looked back to the others. "This spot I'm on is very thick, almost right up to the hole."

He hung his head over the edge and called out for Hugo. There was no answer. He tried again and again got no response. He stared down into the hole for a bit, then crawled back a bit and sat up.

"There's something down there," he called back to the group.

"What do you mean?" Rose said.

"There's a cavern down there over a hundred feet deep. I can't see it well, but there's a building or something down there. Looks like it's surrounded by water."

"That doesn't make sense," Rick said. "How can someone build something inside a sealed volcano?"

"Perhaps it wasn't always sealed," Virginia said. "Maybe there was an opening facing the cove, and the landslide covered it. Hiding his treasure trove inside an extinct volcano would appeal to Blackbeard's sense of theater."

"And maybe be another level of protection if someone did stumble across the island," Rick said. "Maybe Blackbeard had an entire operations base set up here."

"Nice idea," Rose said. "But we'd need to get down there to find out."

"We can do that," Rick said. "We'll tie this rope off to the boulder, drop the end into the hole, and down we go."

"Climb down a rope a hundred feet?" Rose said. "Maybe. Climb back up? Forget it. I'd never make it."

"Damien, Gustave and I will climb back up first. The three of us can pull you and Virginia back up."

“I don’t know about this,” Rose said.

“This could be the greatest Blackbeard find in history,” Virginia said. “I’ll take the risk.”

“I don’t know about the rest of you,” Damien said, “but I’m going down there. That building must be full of treasure.”

“I’m not leaving the treasure on this island,” Gustave said.

“The votes are in,” Rick said. “Looks like we’re going, Rosie.”

“I’m reminding you all,” Rose said, “that the last group decision like this got people killed.”

Rick turned to the rest of them. “Okay, one at a time, use the rope to help you down to that boulder. I’ll keep it anchored. I’ll be last, bring the rope with me, and then we’re going into an extinct volcano.”

Rose sighed. “This had better be worth it.”

One by one, the group worked their way down to the hole in the crater floor. Rick was the last to make the trip, dragging the rope behind him. Once he made it to the bottom, he tied the end around the boulder. Then he crawled over to the edge of the hole beside Damien.

Rick peered in. The light from the hole in the crater lit the area right below him. It seemed like the rope would be long enough to get to the bottom. The cavern looked just as Damien had described. There was a patch of ground under the opening, littered with the huge shards from the broken crater floor. Water lapped against the shards, and further out in that water, out of the direct light from the opening, rose the shadow of a large structure. The broken rifle and Hugo’s body lay straight down below him. Hugo wasn’t moving.

Hugo surviving the fall would have been impossible. Rick thought he’d try and spare Damien some of that initial emotional impact by going first and moving the corpse into the shadows. “You follow me down.”

"No, I'll go," Damien said. "I saw the building first."

Damien seemed unfazed by Hugo's twisted corpse, or even concerned about his man's death once he'd seen what he thought could be the treasure vault.

"Okay, then," Rick said. "Go ahead."

Damien positioned himself at the edge as the other four resumed their braking positions on the rope.

*"Laissez les bon temps rouler,"* Damien said.

The four lowered him down hand over hand. Rick was so nervous about not letting Damien plummet to the ground that he had to keep reminding himself to breathe. His other worry was that he'd estimated the depth of the cavern wrong, and the rope might come up short. After what seemed like an eternity, the rope went slack. They'd had five feet to spare.

"Thank God," Rose said.

Rick dropped the rope and crawled over to the edge. He looked down to see Damien untying the rope around his waist. He didn't even glance at Hugo. Then he walked over to the edge of the water and peered over at the structure.

"*Mère de Dieu,*" he gasped, and then returned to the bottom of the rope.

"You will not believe it," he called up. "This is no building down here. It's a pirate ship."

# CHAPTER SEVENTEEN

Damien was right. Rose could not believe what she heard. There were a half-dozen reasons she could immediately come up with for why there would not be a two-hundred-year-old pirate ship inside an extinct volcano. But the excitement of finding such a historical artifact trumped her rational dismissal of Damien's discovery.

If she thought she was excited, Virginia looked over the moon thrilled. Anticipation lit her face like a lighthouse signal.

"One of the lost ships!" Virginia said. "Blackbeard set sail with four and came back with one. And we've found one!"

She went to the rope, clasped it with both hands, and leaned over the side. Rose grabbed her at the waist and pulled her back in.

"Hold it!" she said. "Damien hasn't seen what else is down there yet."

Virginia wormed free, and then disappeared over the side.

"There's no stopping her," Rick said. "Gustave, you're next."

Gustave nodded and descended on the rope.

"That's a long way down," Rose said.

"There's shards of hardened lava to break your fall, if that makes you feel any better."

"Somehow it doesn't. I'll never get back up."

Rick put an arm around her waist. "I guarantee I'll get you out of that cavern. I could never leave you behind. But you can stay up here if you want to. I mean it's boiling hot in the sun, and it's only a tiny bit likely the iguanas will crawl up here. But seriously, do you really want to hang back, now that we've found what we've been looking for?"

"We discovered something. It may not be what we were looking for."

Then she had the bad feeling that it could actually be what they'd been looking for, and they'd wish they hadn't found it.

She grabbed the rope. "I know I'm going to regret this."

"You said that when you put on your engagement ring, and look how wrong you were about that."

Rose grabbed the rope in both hands and leaned out over the side. Her heart beat a mile a minute. She uttered a whispered curse about her husband, and began her descent. Her long climb down kept her pulse pounding the entire time. The three-way balancing act between tired arm muscles trying to hold her weight, cramping thigh muscles trying to slow her descent, and warming palms from the friction of the rope, kept her certain she was about to plummet to the ground at any moment.

The lower she dropped, the thicker the air became, a humid blanket that smelled of minerals with hints of sulfur. The idea that this was the first time fresh air had entered the cavern in two hundred years was hard to believe.

After what felt like an hour, her feet finally touched the ground. She was quite thankful that Gustave had moved Hugo's body off into the shadows and she hadn't landed on it. Rose let go of the rope and staggered out of the way across slabs of the lava lake. She imagined Rick sliding down in one drop like a movie swashbuckler and didn't want him to land on her.

Her eyes had adapted to the darkness as she made the descent, and she could see around the cavern much better. The crescent of ground all of them stood on was made up entirely of small, rounded stones. The still waters here had certainly once been connected to the cove, and wave action had polished the rocks fallen from the volcano's walls over the centuries. That confirmed that the opening had been here for ages before any pirate made landfall.

Along the water's edge, the thin, white shells of small crabs dotted the shoreline. She was amazed that something managed to survive here in what had been almost total darkness.

Still water filled most of the rest of the cavern. Two-thirds of the cavern walls were what was left of the magma tube that had fed the volcano, black stone with an uneven surface. In places where the lava had paused its retreat, there were rings around the walls like the dirt left in an unclean bath tub. The third of the wall farthest away was made up of the backside of the avalanche that bisected the cove. A handful of slivers of light peered through tiny gaps between the stones.

In the center of all this stood a tall ship. It faced Rose bow on, with a dozen yards between the bowsprit and the water's edge. She took out her flashlight and shined a beam on the ship for a better look. The ship looked to be about a hundred feet long and twenty-five feet wide. Cannons still stuck from the gunwale ports along the side. The wood on the hull was nearly black, though Rose didn't know if it had been that color to begin with. The name on the bow read *Avarice*. That confirmed it. That had been the name Blackbeard had given one of his captured ships.

She'd ended her life here with two masts, but all the rigging had rotted away, and without that support, the masts and yard arms had collapsed. The forward of the two were missing, leaving just an eight-foot remnant jutting from the deck. The remaining center mast had snapped and lay with one end on crushed deck railings and the other in the water. A set of cabins rose at the ship's stern, and one more as the foc'sle in the bow before the forward mast. The ship rode low in the water and listed several degrees to port. She'd either been damaged in the avalanche or sprung a leak over time, but she was clearly resting on the bottom.

Rick arrived at the cavern floor and then bounded up beside Rose.

"Well, will you look at that," he said. "An honest-to-God pirate ship."

"This makes no sense," Rose said. "Think of all the antique furniture we've seen rotted away, even though it had been stored in a dry place. There's no way this ship should still be standing after two hundred years in the water."

"And yet," Rick said, "here it is."

Damien, Gustave, and Virginia joined Rick and Rose. Virginia gazed at the ship like she was having a religious experience.

"After all these years," she whispered. "Trapped so long in darkness, and now to be brought back into the light of day."

Damien's face was flushed with pure excitement. "Blackbeard came back to North Carolina with no treasure and short one ship. If we found the ship, I'm going to bet we've found the treasure."

Rick nodded, and then smiled. "There's only one way to find out."

"Rick," Rose said, "that boat can't possibly be safe to walk on."

"If it's still supporting all those cannons, I think it can support little old us."

"I don't see any boats here to ferry us over," Rose said.

"It's a short swim."

"Swim it?" Virginia said.

"I could go first," Gustave said, "then climb up inside through one of the gunwale ports."

"He swims like a fish," Damien said. "He'll make sure it's safe, then we can follow him over."

"And if there's treasure there," Rose said, "how would we even get it off the boat and out of there?"

Rick put his arm around her waist. "Rosie, I've found in situations like this, it doesn't pay to think that far ahead."

"No, not thinking ahead is what *gets* you in situations like this."

"Start swimming, Gustave," Damien said.

The crewman kicked off his shoes and tied them around his neck. He waded into the water.

"Damn," he said. "This is cold."

"Don't be *un bébé*," Damien said.

Gustave grinned, and then dove into the water. He began to cross the gap to the boat with bold, powerful strokes.

"Damien didn't oversell the man's swimming skills," Rick said.

To the sailor's left, the surface of the water seemed to make a bulge a few feet across, then it subsided. Rose's heart skipped a beat.

"Did you see that?" she said.

"See what?"

Rose shined her flashlight on the water, but nothing was there.

Gustave reached the boat. He grabbed the lower edge of a gunwale port, turned, and waved to the group with a smile.

"See, the best swimmer," Damien said. "He could outrace a gator, that boy could."

Gustave screamed. His face went white and he pulled himself waist-high out of the water. "There's something in there!"

"Get out of the water," Damien shouted.

Gustave tried to pull himself out. He barely moved. "My legs…I can't move my legs."

Then white foam bubbled from his lips. His eyes rolled up in his head as his body shook. Then his grip on the ship relaxed, and he dropped into the water with a splash. He did not resurface.

Around the ship, faint, pulsing yellow glows lit up in the water. They slowly converged on the spot where Gustave had gone under.

"What the hell?" Rick climbed up on a boulder for a better view.

Rose followed him up. From the top, she had a much better view of the amber lights around the ship. Rick sent his flashlight beam at the area where the pulsing was brightest.

The beam lit up a group of huge jellyfish, feeding off Gustave's corpse.

# CHAPTER EIGHTEEN

Rose and the others aimed their beams near where Rick's lit the water.

Each enormous jellyfish measured at least four feet across. Tentacles spread out from their bottoms and wrapped around Gustave's corpse. Between the multiple jellyfish and the spaghetti of tendrils it was hard to gauge how long they were, but many strands stretched out well past the flashlights' beams. At the center of the jellyfish's clear body pulsed a glowing, yellow-green mass.

"*Mère de Dieu*," whispered Damien. "Sea wasps. Very dangerous at normal size. But those are huge."

"It's as if they are protecting the ship," Rose said.

"They *are* protecting the ship," Virginia said. "Look at the cavern walls."

She shined her flashlight at the wall near them. It spotlighted a carved symbol that looked like a combination of a spiral overlaid with an inverted cross crowned by a pentagram. Virginia turned her beam to a second location where the same symbol had been carved.

"The symbols encircle the cavern," she continued. "These are potent symbols in the dark arts. They can amplify a spell cast in the center of them. Justinia Florescu cast the spell to protect the ship and its contents from onboard the ship itself."

"Justinia who?" Rick said.

"The witch Blackbeard brought to the island."

Rose thought it was odd that this was the first time Virginia had referenced the mythical witch's name.

"Giant killer jellyfish, symbols of witchcraft, and the creatures we encountered on the way here," Virginia said. "Is all of this finally enough to have you believe this powerful woman was here?"

Rose had to admit all the evidence of the witch's existence and potency was overwhelming. The witchcraft she had practiced worked. After three attacks by giant creatures, there was no telling what other traps the witch had set.

"All we've seen says the witch was here," Rick said. "And all of these defenses prove that the treasure Blackbeard hid is on that ship. Otherwise, why bother?"

"Rick! You still want to go over there?"

"One thing I've always found true is that you can't look a run of good luck in the mouth. Mine will get us to the treasure on that ship. It got us this far."

"Your run of luck did not rub off on any of my crew," Damien said.

"Luck is nonsense," Virginia said. "We all made it this far because we were destined to do so. The culmination of my life's work is within reach. We can't walk away from it. I won't walk away."

"Virginia has a point," Rick said. "Now that we're here…" Rick pointed to the boat, "…it would be crazy to not go there."

"Walking across a two-hundred-year-old shipwreck is risky enough," Rose said. "Add in fighting some supernatural curse and the risk isn't worth it."

"We can't go home empty-handed," Rick said. "We've already spent a lot to get here."

Rose knew that tone in Rick's voice meant he was about to confess a grievous sin. She hated that tone. "What do you mean, 'spent'?"

"Um." Rick fidgeted. "Someone had to fuel up Humphrey's plane to get us here, and fill that envelope he gave to Damien. That someone was our savings account."

Anger sent Rose's blood pressure soaring. "What? That cushion protects us from going out of business. How could you gamble that?"

"It isn't gambling if it's a sure thing." Rick gestured to the ship. "And the sure thing is sitting right there."

Rose clenched her fists in fury. "If we live to get out of this, you are going to regret you did."

"When we get out of this rich, you're going to regret you doubted me."

"We still can't get to the ship," Damien said.

Rick looked around the area. He shined his light on the fallen mast. "There. Nature has made us a gangplank."

"Except that it doesn't go all the way to the shore here," Rose said. "And even setting foot in that water probably attracts a sea wasp."

"We'll make a little causeway to it," Virginia said. "We'll grab some of the larger rocks here, and make a little path over to the downed mast."

"I like it," Rick said.

"It's worth a try," Damien said. "I can practically smell treasure on that ship."

Rose felt like she was the only one of them with any common sense left. "That mast won't support your weight, Rick. Not after all these years in the water."

"We won't find out until I get to it. And we can't get to it without a causeway. Follow my lead."

Rose shook her head. At no point had following Rick's lead ever been safe and secure.

Rick hefted up a good-sized rock and walked it over to the two-yard gap between the shore and the fallen mast. He heaved it into the water and it landed with a splash a few feet away. The impact attracted big, luminous sea wasps on both sides.

"That motion gathered an unwelcome audience," Rose said. "Just like Gustave's swimming. Fall in that water and they'll be waiting for you."

"My number one reason for not falling in." Rick went for another rock.

Virginia and Damien grabbed some stones and dropped them into the water. Rose sighed and joined the little work detail. They made a pile at the water's edge that stuck out of the water and soon stretched almost to the mast. When it got five feet from its goal, Rick took a position at the end and the group passed him the rocks one at a time to finish the bridge. When he finally laid the last stone in place, an irregular little causeway poked out of the water's surface almost all the way to the mast. The water on both sides glowed from the sea wasps the activity had attracted.

"Here goes," Rick said.

He stepped out to the final rock, then leaned forward to rest against the fallen mast. The palms of his hands touched the pole. He looked puzzled. He slapped the pole with one hand.

"This isn't wood," he called back. "It feels like cold, hard rock made to look like wood."

"It can't be," Damien said. "You can't sail a stone ship."

"Maybe the witch turned it to stone," Rick said, "like Medusa in the old myths."

"You would be best served to not mock the magic you don't understand," Virginia said.

Rose bent down and sniffed the water again. "It's not magic. It's science. This water is loaded with all sorts of minerals. The ship absorbed them over time, displacing the moisture in the wood. The ship is now petrified wood. That's how it can still be here at all."

"Then climbing this should be a breeze." The others shined their lights on the mast. Rick scrambled up the pole on all fours. Just short of the deck, he stood straight up and turned around at the waist.

"Easy as pie," he said.

One foot slipped. Rick flailed his arms for balance and failed. He toppled off the mast.

Rose caught her breath.

At the last second, Rick grabbed the edge of the deck rail. His body slammed into the hull with his feet just above the water. He groaned. Several jellyfish rose to the water's surface beneath him. Rose was sure the next thing she'd see was her husband being swarmed, just like Gustave.

Rick did a slow-motion pullup, then swung one leg up over the railing. He rolled himself up over the side and hit the deck on his back. After a few deep breaths, he sat up and looked back at the group.

"New safety tip: the end of that mast is a little slick."

Rose was thrilled he was alive, and ready to kill him for being so careless. Rick stood up and beat the deck with the soles of his shoes. "The whole thing seems petrified. Come on over, Rosie."

Rose took a deep breath and began a cautious crossing of the stone causeway. The rocks were not as stable as Rick had made them seem, and the ones that water had splashed were damn slick. Step by step she made her way to the mast. When she arrived, she leaned down and grabbed it with both hands. The surface was cold, hard, and slimy. Under her breath she cursed Rick again for acting like a showoff. With as firm a grip as she could muster, she made her way up the mast on hands and knees, staring only at the bit of the mast in front of her face. Her ascent seemed glacial.

"I have you, Rosie," Rick said.

She looked up to see she was at the ship. Rick grabbed her under her arms, lifted her off the mast and swung her around onto the deck. He set her down and she slapped his face.

"Easy as pie? You idiot."

Rick pouted and gave the side of his face an exaggerated massage where she'd hit him. "In my defense, I was referring to a very complicated pie."

"Just get us out of here alive, okay?"

"Always my plan."

Virginia and Damien made their way across the mast. When the four of them were together, they added their flashlight beams to the light from the volcano's opening and inspected the deck of the ship. Everyone had to lean at a bit of an angle to compensate for the ship's slight list to one side. The ship looked like it hadn't aged since it had run aground. The petrification process had preserved the deck, capstans and the superstructure over the stern. Even the great steering wheel was in one piece, although Rose was certain it would never turn again. Cannons lined the gunwales, ready to be loaded and fired. The wooden carriages were now rock, but the cast iron cannons themselves looked good as new.

But Rose couldn't relish this archeological find, because an awful story was told upon the deck. Scattered about the ship were skeletons, most almost fully articulated. Some lay beside the cannon, others near the railing, even one halfway down the stairway that led to the hold. A pile of bones surrounded the forward mast, as if a number of men had been clustered there when some kind of mass death took the crew.

"Look at these men," Damien said. "All dead at their posts, like something struck them down in an instant."

"Volcanic gasses maybe?" Rose guessed. "They can be toxic."

"But from a dead volcano?" Rick said.

Virginia walked to the bow and faced the shadowy stump of the forward mast. "I see what killed all of these men."

Rose and the rest picked their way through the skeletons and joined her beside the mast. A dark shape bulged at its base. Rose shined her flashlight on the mast. She could not believe what she saw.

The mummified body of a woman in a long, black dress hung on the mast. Gray hair cascaded to her shoulders and her eye sockets were black holes that seemed to open to a void beyond. A pirate's cutlass stuck out of her chest, with the tip likely embedded in the mast behind her. Her mouth hung open in a frozen scream. White teeth sparkled in the flashlight's beam.

"These men died from a witch's curse," Virginia said. "Meet Justinia Florescu."

# CHAPTER NINETEEN

The anguished look on the mummy's face made Rose shudder. The woman had to have died in horrific pain. But the reverential look on Virginia's face as she gazed at the mummy was nearly as scary. This wasn't the look of a satisfied historian. She'd seen obsessed collectors discover the object of their desire in her shop many times. Virginia looked more enchanted by this corpse than any of those people had been with their finds.

"This mummy, it cannot be," Damien said. "The others are skeletons, and she is not?"

"It doesn't make sense at all," Rose said. "Mummification happens in dry climates and this cavern is anything but dry."

"If Blackbeard brought her here to protect the island with a spell," Rick said, "why would he have his men kill her?"

"So the spell would forever be unbroken." Virginia's eyes stayed locked on the mummy's face. Her voice was little more than a whisper. "Only the witch who cast a spell can cast the counter-spell that can break it."

Rose touched Virginia's shoulder. "Virginia?"

Virginia snapped out of her reverie and took a step back from the mast. "Blackbeard would have Justinia cast her last spells from the ship, amplified by the sigils carved into the cavern walls. This way the magic would be strongest when thieves were closest to the treasure. He'd probably ordered his crew to murder her as soon as she cast the spells. Her final act with her last breath was to kill everyone aboard, and I'd guess bring down the avalanche that sealed the treasure from Blackbeard forever."

"That's an awful double-cross," Rick said. He stepped in front of the corpse and reached for the cutlass handle. "We should probably take her down."

He gripped the handle. He shuddered and let it go like it was white hot. "That doesn't feel right."

"What do you mean?' Rose said.

"It's some combination of hot and smarmy and electrically-charged. I don't know what's wrong with it, but I know I don't want to touch it."

"Or Justinia doesn't want you to touch it," Virginia said.

"I think she stopped having any say in that two hundred years ago," Rick said.

Rose knew that normally this would be where Rick would pull out the sword, just to prove he wasn't going to be intimidated. When he didn't, Rose knew there was something exceptionally strange about the blade.

"If events unfolded as you say," Rick said, "then there's treasure on this ship."

"It would make sense to hide a ship full of treasure here instead of burying it," Damien said. "Saves a lot of time and effort."

Rick led them to the steps that went down to the hold. Damien followed him down.

"I'll check the captain's cabin," Rose said as she headed for the stern of the ship.

At the stern, the steering wheel stood on a raised deck surrounded by a U-shape of cabins. She figured that the one in the center would have belonged to the *Avarice's* captain. A skeleton had propped the cabin door open, which was a godsend for Rose. She doubted she'd have been able to move a door made of petrified wood, even if the centuries-old hinges would have allowed it. She stepped into the cabin.

She was the first person to step inside this cabin in two centuries, so she anticipated some exciting historical finds. But what she saw around her was a bit of a disappointment. Everything that hadn't been transformed into petrified wood was either gone or decayed into something unrecognizable. The captain's bunk would have had a mattress and sheets, the windows most certainly would have had drapes. But all of those were bare. Inside an open cupboard, stacks of pewter plates sat on the shelves. She lifted one up and wondered how many pirate meals had been served on it. The plate was a workman-like piece, so even the captain of a pirate ship apparently did not live in luxury.

A chart table stood at the other side of the cabin. Time had claimed all the maps, but a compass and ruler sat on the table, right where they'd been left, when whoever was jammed in the doorway had tried to escape during the witch's spell.

The cabin was interesting, but nothing here smacked of pirate treasure. She hoped Rick was having better luck belowdecks.

Rick needed a tight grip on the banister to keep from slipping down the petrified steps. The first deck he and Damien encountered was a gun deck. Cannons still pointed out the stern, waiting to repel ships that would never come. Racks of cannon balls lined the bulkheads and two stout foot-tall kegs stood sentinel beside every gun.

Damien went over to one of the cannons. "My family comes from men who sailed ships like this for the French Navy and settled in New Orleans. They were gunners and proud of it."

He examined the keg. Unlike the petrified wood of the rest of the ship, the keg had a bumpy, black surface. Damien pulled out his pocket knife and scraped some of the black off the keg lid. The blade exposed wood.

"*Mère de Dieu*," he said. "These are gunpowder kegs, coated in pitch and tar to protect from the elements. Protected so well that the staves have not been turned to stone."

Rick stepped back. "You mean there's two-hundred-year-old gunpowder in those kegs?"

"Yes." Damien took a gentle step back from the keg. "I would not play around with them."

Damien left Rick staring at the keg and disappeared down the steps to the lower deck. Rick wondered if these kegs could all explode without warning and end this little expedition in an instant.

Then Damien's voice drifted back up the passage. "Winner, winner, chicken dinner."

Rick joined him below. The two of them played their flashlights around the aft section of the hold. Stacks of metal boxes lined the bulkheads. Some had overturned and opened. Gold coins and jewelry of all types lay all over the floor. The horde sparkled as the flashlight beams played across them.

"It's really here after all," Damien said. "It's hard to believe."

"What's really hard to believe is that Blackbeard just left treasure lying around on the deck like this."

"Like the rigging, all the cloth or leather bags probably just rotted away," Damien said.

He knelt beside the pile of coins and picked up a handful. He inspected them under the light. "French, English, Spanish, and all dated from the early 1700s. The loot of a pirate who did not play favorites when choosing victims."

"And who knows what else is in the chests," Rick said.

"There's more wealth here than anyone could ever spend."

"I'm willing to rise to that challenge," Rick said.

Damien stuffed his handfuls of coins into his pockets and smiled. “My new good luck pieces.”

Rick couldn’t wait to show this to Rose. Then he realized that Virginia hadn’t followed them down and was still on deck. Could she have thought that creepy corpse was more interesting than Blackbeard’s riches?

# CHAPTER TWENTY

Rose left the cabin and made it to the stairway just as Rick came bounding up out of the hold. She hadn't seen him wearing this big a smile since he'd hit the trifecta at the old Ten Brock Race Course. They met on deck. He grabbed her shoulders and kissed her.

"It's there," he said. "Tens of thousands of dollars, maybe millions, who knows. Boxes of loot waiting for us to take them home."

After finding nothing in the captain's cabin, Rose was glad the ship had given them something for all their trouble, even though it meant there'd be no living with Rick after this. "I suppose this is when you expect me to apologize for ever doubting you and your plan to find pirate treasure?"

"Absolutely. And you can continue to profess your gratitude all the way home."

Damien stepped out onto the deck, flipping a gold coin with one hand. "I have become a very wealthy man."

"How about taking care of the families of your dead crew?" Rose said.

Damien stopped flipping the coin and stared at it in the palm of his hand. "Yes, the families, of course. But there will be plenty left over for me. Going to trade the old shrimper for a yacht. Buy myself a plantation."

Rose searched the deck for Virginia and did not see her. "Virginia?"

Virginia stepped out from behind the forward mast. There was something awkward and artificial about her steps. Maybe it was just the angle of the deck and the slick, petrified planking.

"It's all here," Rick called to her. "Just like the chart room said it would be."

"Of course it is." Virginia smiled, but the grin looked more malevolent than joyful to Rose.

Rose turned back to Rick. "Okay, Bright Boy. Now how do we get this new-found wealth out of this cavern, let alone all the way home?"

Rick glanced down at the deck and gave his moustache a thoughtful stroke. "Yes...well...there's that." He looked across the deck to the rope hanging down through the hole in the volcano crater. "So, we climb out, get back to Humphrey on the boat. Then we bring back what we need to rig a block and tackle. With that we should be able to haul it all out of here with ease."

This time, Rick's attempt to make the impossible seem easy fell flat for Rose. "You think we'll just wander up and down the mountain multiple times, carrying equipment and treasure, with all the giant creatures still out there, and survive?"

"She has a point," Damien said. "We have a boxcar worth of treasure down there."

Rose turned and caught sight of a jellyfish tentacle snaking up over the gunwale. She pointed past Rick's shoulder at it. "Rick!"

Rick spun around. "Oh my God."

"They're everywhere," Damien said.

He was right. Jellyfish tentacles snaked over the sides of the ship's center, from aft of the forward mast to forward of the cabin in the stern. It looked like slick, silver hair had sprouted from the railings.

"Abandon ship," Rick said. "Cross back over the mast."

But it was too late. Tentacles had already stretched out of the water and wound all around the fallen mast. Even if shoes offered protection from the sting, there was no way anyone could balance on the mast with the jellyfish writhing all over it.

Virginia stood at the stub of the forward mast, transfixed by the jellyfish assault.

"Virginia," Rick called out, "head down to the foc'sle. Find something to hide in for protection."

His shout seemed to bring her to her senses. She retreated into the foc'sle on the bow.

"C'mon, everyone," Rick said. "We'll go to the hold. The treasure boxes are pretty big. We'll dump a few and hide inside until these things figure out there's nothing up here worth eating."

Rick led them down the staircase that led to the gundeck and then the hold. Several steps past the gundeck, he stopped short. Further down the staircase, tentacles had already wrapped themselves around the steps. Jellyfish had already invaded the hold.

"Damn it," Rick said. "Back to the gundeck and get to the stern."

The three retreated to a spot between the two cannons facing the open ports in the stern. Behind them, tentacles explored the top of the steps. Others began to enter the gunports along the center of the ship.

Damien searched the area around them. A rammer for the cannons leaned against the bulkhead. He grabbed it and held it across his chest.

"We can't fight them off with that," Rick said.

"We can't fight them off with anything," Rose said. "Nothing short of lighting the ship on fire will do that."

"Or boiling the water they're swimming in," Rick said.

"That would work. Even heating it a little would be enough to disorient them."

"This water was cold from never seeing sunlight." Rick pointed out the firing port in the stern to the avalanche slide. "What if we mixed the water in here with the water out there?"

"That cove water is at least twenty degrees warmer. It would shock these things if not outright kill them. But how do we do that?"

Rick set a hand on a cannon. "We blow a hole in that wall."

Damien's eyes lit up. He patted a tar-encased keg by the cannon. "Yes. The gunpowder."

Rick pointed at the cannonballs along the wall. "And the cannonballs."

"Are you insane?" Rose said. "You want to use two-hundred-year-old cannons to blow up a rock wall?"

"You bet. We'll kill these jellyfish, *and* Humphrey can sail the shrimper right in through the new hole and we can load the treasure. All our problems are solved."

As far as Rose was concerned, all their problems would grow exponentially. Crushed by an avalanche, killed by an exploding cannon, smothered by this stone ship shaking apart. She could make a damn long list.

"Rosie," Rick said. "We don't have time to try anything else. Sometimes you've got to bet big on your last hand to salvage a losing game."

Further up the ship, tentacles now explored the stairway going up to the main deck. From amidships up as far as Rose's light could illuminate, the deck was a mass of pulsing, silver tentacles.

Rick didn't wait for her to answer. "Damien, you know how to load one of these things?"

"You'd be surprised what you learn in my line of work." He tried to roll the cannon forward. "Be better if we could get these sticking out of the firing port. But these wheels are not moving. That also means no recoil. Expect to shatter the carriage."

Rose had a feeling they were all about to die. She looked back at the tentacles. They'd already crossed half the distance to the stern.

Damien popped the stopper from the bunghole on a gunpowder keg. He carried it to the front of the cannon barrel and poured a healthy charge of it into the cannon's mouth. Rick kicked a cannonball loose and carried it over to Damien. He moved to put it in the gun barrel.

"Not yet." Damien pulled off his shirt and tore it in half. He wadded one half up and stuffed it in the barrel. Then he used the rammer to pack the whole thing down. "Now!"

Rick rolled the cannonball into the muzzle. Damien shoved the other half of his shirt into the cannon and packed that down as well.

"Almost done," he said. "We do the same on this other one."

Rose tore her eyes away to check the tentacle progress. They were only a few yards away. "Those things are getting really close."

Damien looked up at the tentacles as he poured gunpowder into the second cannon. "Damn."

He finished pouring. Rick stripped off his shirt and handed it to Damien.

"Trade you for matches," he said to Damien.

Damien handed Rick a box of matches and began to duplicate the loading process on the other gun. Rick hoisted up the gunpowder keg and dashed to a spot between them and the advancing jellyfish. He poured a line of gunpowder across the width of the deck, then another line from that one back to where Rose stood. He took a match from the box and handed it to Rose.

"If those things get to that line," he said, "light the match and touch the flame to the gunpowder. The flash and flame ought to buy us a little time."

Rose stared at the match in her hand, then at the grainy line on the deck between her and the jellyfish. Was she really supposed to save the day by igniting ancient gunpowder?

"Will that work?" she said.

"Sure. They do it in the movies all the time."

"The movies?"

Rick was gone before she could tell him how stupid this plan was.

He returned to help Damien at the cannons. Damien pulled out rolling papers, and with the same expertise he'd displayed with tobacco earlier, he now made two sealed paper cylinders filled with gunpowder.

The first of the tentacles crossed the gunpowder line. Rose's heart jumped into her throat.

"Rick?" Rose said.

Rick glanced back at the mass of writhing tentacles. "Light it up!"

More tentacles crossed the line. Rose struck the match, then knelt and touched the flame to the gunpowder.

The powder ignited with a flash and a pop. Grain lit grain and a line of flame ripped across the stone deck. Fire hit the main line and raced out along it in both directions.

The running flame hit the jellyfish tentacles. The tentacles shuddered and jumped off the deck. Searing flames left dark, black lines across them. The fire burned right through some and left the severed tips on Rose's side of the fire line. Rose stifled a shout of victory as the flash fire snuffed out.

Damien wedged the homemade fuses into the touchholes of the cannons. "These are going to burn damn fast. Light it and get out of the way."

The tentacles that had tangled with the gunpowder retreated. But there were plenty more where those came from. A new wave rolled over the scorched line on the deck. Rose's heart sank.

"Here they come again!" Rose said.

Rick handed a match to Damien. "Let 'em rip."

Rose moved to the corner of the ship away from the cannon. Rick and Damien slashed their matches across the cannon bodies. Two matchheads flared to life. Both men touched the fuses and they exploded into little sizzling sticks. Damien ran for the far bulkhead. Rick ran for Rose.

Rick reached her, pressed her down to the deck, and lay on top of her. "Two-to-one this is going to be loud."

Then just a fraction of a second apart, two huge booms shook the cabin.

# CHAPTER TWENTY-ONE

As the cannon balls rocketed through the firing ports, the petrified gun carriages shattered. With the barrels on the inside of the firing ports, a cloud of smoke enveloped the cabin. The shockwave of the explosions hit the bulkhead instead of rolling out across the cavern. The ceiling shattered into a blizzard of shards and stone splinters. Cracks ripped across the stern and added another shower of petrified chunks to the storm. The deck shifted beneath Rick and it seemed the whole ship was about to collapse.

Debris pounded his back and sent needles of pain up and down his spine. But all he worried about was Rose. After he'd lit the fuse, he'd dived on top of her, determined to add himself as a level of protection from the imminent danger. But he'd underestimated its magnitude and he couldn't see how she could have survived this unscathed.

The rain of rock ceased. The ship went still. Rick opened his eyes and shined his flashlight around the cabin.

Dust still hung thick in the air, but he could see that the stern bulkhead had folded in and the ceiling above it had collapsed. Had they been any closer to the stern they would have been crushed by the petrified timbers. The debris blocked any hope of a view of the cavern. But the rest of the ship held fast. The sharp taste of spent gunpowder coated Rick's mouth. He pushed himself to his knees over Rose and wiped the worst of the dirt from his face. His ears rang like a sustained church bell.

He laid a hand on Rose's shoulder. "Rosie, you okay?"

Rose had curled into a ball where the bulkhead met the deck. Her hands covered her ears. She didn't move and Rick's first panicked thought was that she had died. Then her back flexed as she took a deep breath. She turned and looked up at him with the blue eyes he'd been in love with since the day they met.

"I'm fine," she said. "No need to shout."

Rick didn't realize he'd shouted. He could barely hear himself speak. He reached down and offered her his hand to help her up. With a tug, he got her to her feet.

Damien stepped out of the haze from the other side of the cabin, coughing. "Everyone okay?"

Rick nodded. Then his heart jumped as he remembered the tentacles that were consuming the ship. He spun around and shined his light forward. He couldn't see much further than the scorched line the burning gunpowder had charred across the deck. But that was enough to let his pulse slow down. There wasn't a tentacle to be seen. The blast must have sent the jellyfish packing.

The dust settled and cleared the view forward. The three of them moved up to the gunpowder line. The blast had done far more than scare the jellyfish. It had obliterated them. Beyond the scorch line, a puree of tentacles coated the deck and bulkheads.

"We splattered 'em," Rick said.

"Why are you shouting?" Damien said.

Rick pointed to his ear. "Ringing!"

"You didn't cover your ears?" Damien said.

"I'll remember to next time I shoot cannons on a pirate ship."

"Let's see if this plan worked." Damien led them to the slimy stairway to the main deck.

As Rose fell in behind Rick, she stopped him with a tug on his belt. "Rick, your back."

Rick glanced over his shoulder. Stripping off his shirt had left him no protection from the blast debris. Blood ran from numerous scrapes and punctures. Now that he saw that, the pain that accompanied the injuries arrived to back up what his eyes told him.

"I may be sleeping face-down for a while," he said.

"There are a few big pieces here. Want me to get them out?"

"Pluck me like a chicken." He handed her his flashlight.

Rick watched over his shoulder as Rose extracted several bits of stone from his back. Each removal came with an unpleasant sharp pain. After the fourth bit, she stopped. "That's all the ones I can see. There may be small bits embedded deeper."

Damien looked back from the base of the stairway. "You going to survive?"

"Maybe you can hook me up with a fine bayou doctor when we get back," Rick said.

Damien smiled. "You'd be surprised by the number of doctors I have on call in my line of work."

The three of them climbed to the top of the stairs. Dust swirled in the air, but even with that there was noticeably more light in the cavern, which gave Rick hope they'd succeeded. The soupy remains of jellyfish tentacles coated the deck. Behind them, the very aft end of the cabin had buckled, but the area as far back as the ship's wheel still looked unscathed. The three climbed the short stairway to the upper deck for a better look at what their two-gun salute had wrought.

The cannonballs had done their job. The brittle lava boulders had shattered on impact. Some may have even been broken by the shockwave. But either way, the mountain of boulders that had blocked the cavern had collapsed. A thick, black cloud of volcanic dust blocked the view beyond the broken wall. A pile of rocks now leaned against the ship's stern.

Down below, sea water rushed in around the sides of that pile and into the cavern floor, which had been several feet below the level of the cove. As the waters churned and mixed, Rose's prediction came true. The glow of the giant jellyfish had disappeared. After untold generations had survived isolated in the cave, either the added daylight or the higher water temperature had killed them. Rick didn't care which, as long as the job had been done.

"See, Rosie," Rick said. "My amazing plan worked, and I'm willing to accept full credit for it."

"Where's Virginia?" Rose said. She spun around and called Virginia's name across the deck.

Virginia stepped out of the foc'sle and gave Rose a relieved, acknowledging wave.

"Look at that opening to the cove," Damien said. "Even Humphrey could sail the shrimper right in here. We walk the treasure down the rocks off the stern and load it onto my *cher bâteau.*"

Just then the rumble of a big engine echoed in the cavern. The silhouette of a boat in the cove appeared in the dust cloud.

"Speak of the Devil," Rick said, "and he shall appear."

The boat came closer as the airborne dust settled. Rick had the awful realization that this ship was not the old shrimper. This sleek boat had a long bow with a simple pilothouse amidships and a small cockpit at the stern. This was the kind of boat rum-runners in the Caribbean had favored before Prohibition's repeal put them out of business. A big V8 engine belched a throaty burble from a flagless stern. The flat, steel gray paint would make it less visible at sea, and Rick didn't trust anyone who wanted their high-speed boat to be less visible at sea.

"Are you going to surprise me by telling me this is one of the friends you made in your line of work?" Rose said to Damien.

"I wish that it was," Damien said.

"They followed us here?" Rose said.

"They couldn't. If they could have seen us, my lookout would have seen them."

The boat's engine surged in reverse and it stopped just as it nudged the pile of rocks that ran up the stern of the pirate ship.

"I wish we had some of the rifles on the shrimper," Rick said.

"I wish we were *with* the rifles on the shrimper," Rose said.

A heavyset older man in a three-piece suit stepped out of the door to the pilothouse and walked up to the bow. An unlit cigar stuck from the corner of his mouth. A stubby fringe of salt-and-pepper hair encircled his bald head. A scar ran around his neck, as if he'd been beheaded at some point and then sewn back together. This wasn't the kind of person Rick wanted to meet in a cave on a deserted island.

"Ahoy there," the man said. "Funny thing, I was sitting in the cove here wondering where pirate treasure might be hidden. Then all of a sudden, this mountain explodes, and inside, like a prize in Cracker Jacks, is a pirate treasure ship."

"Do you know this guy?" Rick said to Damien.

Virginia joined them on the aft deck. "That's Enrico Lasorda."

That name rang an alarm bell for Rick. "Lasorda? Big-time gangster Lasorda?"

"The one and only," Virginia said.

"Who is he?" Rose said.

"Pick a vice and he caters to it all along the southeastern coast," Damien said. "I've spent years staying under his radar."

Two gangsters carrying tommy guns climbed up from the rear cockpit and joined Lasorda on the bow.

"A very wise move, Damien," Lasorda said. "And you would have stayed that way except for the Sinclairs."

"We didn't tell you where we were going," Rick said.

"No." Lasorda pointed to Virginia. "She did."

Rose spun around to face Virginia. "You? How?"

"She left me a note in her car once she knew where you were flying. In the bayou, she left another message telling me where you were sailing."

"You went to my beautiful home?" Damien said.

"It's not so beautiful anymore," Lasorda said.

Virginia backed away for the stairway. Rick saw the furious look on Rose's face and knew exactly why.

"Virginia's been working for me for years," Lasorda said. "Looking for Blackbeard's treasure. Finally, all that time and money spent on her has paid off."

Rick knew that when you held a bad hand, the only hope was to bluff. "We're not here alone. We brought a big crew with us."

Lasorda motioned to the cabin. One of his thugs exited, pulling Humphrey with him. Rope bound Humphrey's wrists.

"You mean this crew of one?" Lasorda said. "I don't think you can count on him."

"Sorry, Rick," Humphrey said. "There were too damn many of 'em."

Rick figured it was time to double down on the lying. "You made the trip for nothing. There's no treasure here."

"You saying there's a pirate treasure ship, but no treasure?"

"There's treasure," Virginia said. "Check the stern of the ship."

One of the tommy gun men kicked at a rope ladder on the bow. It unrolled down the hull to the base of the rock pile. The gangster beside Humphrey kept his machine gun at the ready and aimed at the three people standing on the *Avarice's* deck. Lasorda and the two men descended down the ladder onto the rock pile and then began to climb up.

"Maybe he'll slip down there and break his neck," Rose said.

"We can always hope," Rick replied. "And Virginia joining him wouldn't hurt my feelings at all."

The two thugs made it on deck. Lasorda climbed over the railing last. His expensive leather shoes slipped on the petrified planks, but he steadied himself at the railing and smiled.

"Sal," he told one man, "you stay on deck with that gun trained on these three. Any excuse is a good excuse to pull the trigger. Frankie, you stick with me."

Then Virginia led Lasorda and Frankie down below decks.

"I can't believe she betrayed us," Rose said.

"Next time I tell you I've spotted a weasel," Rick said, "take my word for it."

# CHAPTER TWENTY-TWO

Lasorda strutted as he headed for the steps to go below decks. He'd known that his treasure search would pay off big time, and he was about to be proven right.

The other bosses had derided his hunt for Blackbeard's treasure. Always they came at him with the pirate jokes, the witch jokes. They had stopped ridiculing his southeast operation when they started begging for South American imports. They were about to stop ridiculing finding pirate treasure.

Virginia led Lasorda and his tommy gun-toting henchman Frankie down into the hold. Light through the missing stern windows was more than enough to illuminate the room.

"I think you were looking for this?" she said.

He stepped onto the deck and his jaw dropped. His cigar hit the deck.

The glorious sight before him was beyond words. Gold coins, silver plates, and religious-themed artifacts lay on the deck the way chickenfeed covered the ground outside a coop. Metal chests lined the bulkheads, promising even more riches within.

Lasorda knelt down and picked up a handful of coins. He poured them from one hand to the other. This was *his* kind of money. Hard and cold.

"Blackbeard himself may have been the last person to touch these coins," he said. "Now they pass on to me, who built an empire bigger than Blackbeard could have even dreamed of. Frankie, check out one of the chests."

His man didn't move. He just stared at the loot with wide eyes.

"Now!" Lasorda said.

"Right, boss."

Frankie went forward, stepping around the riches on the floor. He stepped up to one box and aimed his tommy gun at the old lock that secured it.

"No, idiot!" Lasorda shouted. "You want to kill us? Its two hundred years old. Just smash it."

The gunman cringed. Then he raised the tommy gun and struck the lock with the buttstock. The old iron lock shattered. The man opened the chest.

Within the box sparkled a mound of jewelry. Gem stones of all colors, mountings of silver and gold. Necklaces and rings and tiaras. All this had likely been plundered from wealthy passengers on dozens of ships over time. They lay in an unceremonious heap, stored with as much regard as a mother has tossing children's toys into a toybox. Each piece had been worth quite a bit back then. Each was worth a fortune now.

Lasorda turned to Virginia. "You were right. Those fools led us straight to the lost treasure."

"You supporting my years of work has paid off," Virginia said.

Lasorda scoffed. "You kidding me? All that gave me was zip. These two wandered in with a map, that's what got us here. Makes me second guess what your cut oughta be."

Normally, his attempts to change a deal after the fact raised howls of disapproval. Virginia didn't say a word. Lasorda liked it when a woman knew her place.

"I never wanted to find this place for the treasure," Virginia said. "It was all about finding the ship. I'm going to tend to it while you pack up all this."

Lasorda stifled a laugh. He wouldn't even have to kill her to keep her cut of the treasure. "Sure, you go do that."

Virginia went up the stairs and headed in the direction of the forward mast.

Lasorda turned back to Frankie. "You and the boys are going to have to move all this loot to the boat. I don't want none of it dropped, and I don't want no inventory shrinkage neither."

Lasorda stepped over to the stern and looked out at his boat and the waters of the cove beyond. "This is a hell of a place Blackbeard found. Been going to waste for two hundred years. This could be a new base of operations for me. International waters, no jurisdiction. My own personal kingdom."

A hundred plans whirled through his mind at once. He saw himself as boss of the bosses, financed by the treasure that sat at his feet. He stuffed the coins in his pockets.

"Let's get this treasure moved," he said.

"The Sinclairs?" Frankie said.

"Don't kill 'em yet. Come to think of it, might as well use 'em to help load all this up. Add a little insult to injury. Then we'll finish 'em off when they're of no value anymore."

Frankie grabbed a chest and tried to lift it. It didn't budge.

"I'll send down Sal."

Lasorda went back above deck wearing a triumphant smile. He looked over at Damien and the Sinclairs, who looked mired in despair. That made him smile brighter.

"Hoo, boy!" he said. "Now that's a lot of loot! So selfish of you all to try and keep it all for yourselves. Now your punishment's gonna be ending up with none of it."

#

Virginia had gone straight to the forward mast and now stood before the witch's desiccated corpse. She stared into the empty eye sockets. Virginia ran her fingertips down the gray, papery skin stretched tight over the woman's arms.

She understood how so few people ever got to a moment like this, an instant where a family member's spirit could be put to rest.

Her family was Roma, or Gypsy as most of the world called them. They settled in the New World just like the others in the 1700s, looking for escape from persecution. But persecution always followed the Roma with a bloodhound's resolve. Justinia had been forced into Blackbeard's service, compelled to cast spells for him with the promise of a freedom that never came.

From the moment she did not return from Blackbeard's last voyage, the family began a quest for her. Generations searched down dead ends trying to disprove the ignominy of seeming to have served pirates. But Virginia had dedicated her life to finding Justinia, because she knew the witch's soul would still be waiting. All her work, and the map provided by the clueless Sinclairs, had finally brought Virginia to exactly where she'd longed to be. As soon as Virginia had set foot in the cavern of the pirate ship, she'd felt the presence of Justinia's tortured soul.

"I'm here, Justinia. The family never stopped searching for you. We have never forsaken you. Now I'm here to free you and take you home to rest."

*And share the secrets of all your power,* she wanted to add. Because once she had Justinia's spirit back to Charleston, that would be the price Virginia would demand before letting her relative leave this earthly realm.

Murdered witches rarely passed over to the next stage of life, intent on exacting revenge for their death. Justinia had died with an unsurpassed thirst for revenge, a desire so strong it had kept her soul fueled over centuries of waiting. Her soul had remained tethered to her body, refusing to pass to the beyond.

Virginia gripped the cutlass handle. She felt the life force of the witch hum within it, the same life force that had preserved her body and her dress. Justinia's soul was still here. But the time had come to make sure that it wasn't for much longer.

Virginia reached over and pulled out a medallion that hung from Justinia's neck which the dress had concealed. The circular, brass piece had originally been about two inches across and engraved with a crescent moon with a jagged line between both endpoints, the same witch's symbol from the corner of the map. The bottom third of it had been broken off.

Virginia knelt on the ground, pricked her finger, and drew a special witch's symbol at the corpse's feet. It was not the same symbol on the cavern wall, nor the same symbol she'd drawn on the ground to help drive the iguanas away. This one was two overlapping circles with a pentagram where the circles intersected. This symbol was for a liberating spell.

From around her own neck, Virginia pulled a partial medallion. The ragged edge matched the broken edge of the one around the witch's neck.

"You left this medallion with your daughter," Virginia said, "promising that it would be reunited with yours. She passed it down to her daughter and it continued to be passed down for generations. Now we will make that happen. I'll free you from this earthly prison, and guide you to the peace you deserve."

Virginia fit the two pieces back together and clasped them between her hands. She whispered the liberating spell she'd learned from the ancient family grimoire. The power she'd felt buzz in the cutlass now thrummed hard between her palms. It was as if this witch's spirit, trapped here for so long, sensed freedom was near.

And Virginia's price for that freedom would seem like a bargain.

She repeated the spell and pressed the pieces more firmly together. The completed disk heated up and light began to glow from between her fingers. The warmth grew to an uncomfortable heat. The medallion began to shake her hands back and forth. The metal seared her skin.

Then she felt more than the power, she felt a presence. A consciousness old beyond measure, tainted by death and despair. It awakened like a lion, standing and stretching muscles that for centuries had been bound in place. And as this consciousness became fully awake, one overriding emotion emanated from it like heat from a blast furnace. It was not the gratitude Virginia expected over its rescue. It was boiling revenge.

Virginia feared her plan would not work. This wasn't a compliant spirit that would do Virginia's bidding in return for its freedom. Instead, it seethed within the medallion, consumed not with a desire for eternal peace, but with an obsession for vengeance. Two centuries had not dulled the witch's pain, they had sharpened it. Virginia doubted she would be strong enough to keep such power contained.

Virginia released the medallion. The sensation of the witch's presence lessened, but did not disappear. The liberation spell was still at work, like rushing water scouring away a foundation. When the witch's soul ripped free of her body, she'd tear apart anyone trying to take this ill-gotten treasure. And Virginia wasn't too sure that, in her fury, the witch would spare the one who freed her.

Panic swept through her. The shallowness of her witchcraft skills became painfully obvious. She did not know how to stop what she had started. Of the few spells she knew, the only one that might help would be a barrier spell, but it needed to enhance a solid barrier to work.

She dashed into the foc'sle and soon spied an empty metal chest like the ones in the stern filled with treasure. Virginia dragged it across the deck and set it next to the mast beneath the witch's corpse. This close, she could feel the growing power of the witch's soul the way one felt a blast of wind at a thunderstorm's approach.

She grabbed the cutlass and pulled. It didn't move from the petrified wood of the mast. She braced her feet against the box and pulled harder. Still nothing.

She pushed the handle sideways. The blade bent to one side. The old, fragile metal moaned and then snapped. She almost fell on her face when it broke. She straightened up to see the witch's body still hanging on the mast. The ropes that had bound her had long rotted away, the sword that pinned her to the mast was gone. What was holding her in place?

The rising power of the witch's spirit sent a surge of adrenaline through Virginia. She took the broken sword and wedged the tip between the witch's arm and the mast. The witch was partially fused to the petrified wood. Using the blade as a lever, she pried at the witch's arm. It broke away and hit the deck with a thud.

In a panic, Virginia worked at the rest of the body, chopping and scraping. Limbs fell and with a final effort the torso and head dropped down straight into the box. Virginia gathered the other limbs. The dried skin and hollowed bones felt like paper stretched over the frame of a kite. They also felt warm. Touching them made her skin crawl.

Virginia knew she was in way over her head. She threw the limbs into the box.

She slammed the lid shut and latched the clasp. Virginia drew the symbol for a barrier spell in the dirt on the top of the lid. She lit a match from her pocket and dropped it in the center of the symbol. The spell demanded she use a burning candle, but this was going to have to be good enough.

Something thumped inside the box.

Virginia's mind went blank. She could not remember the barrier spell, or any spell for that matter. All she could think about was getting as far away from this witch and this island as quickly as possible. Then the spell came back to her. She chanted it three times, finishing just as the lighted match went out.

The box thumped a few more times, but then went still.

She sighed in relief. That was way too close for comfort. She would have to take Justinia's bones away from here, to someplace far from the events that caused her death, maybe all the way home to the Carolinas. There Justinia would see the light, and free of the negative energy here, surely she would agree to share all of witchcraft's lost secrets with Virginia before she went to the Great Beyond.

Virginia headed back to where Lasorda stood on the deck by the hold. The bastard could take all the treasure as far as she was concerned. All she needed to get home was that one box.

As Virginia spoke to Lasorda, she could not see the seam between the lid and the box begin to glow green. The line of light pulsed, and with each pulse, its intensity increased.

# CHAPTER TWENTY-THREE

From beside the pilothouse of Lasorda's boat, Humphrey watched the gangsters tromp around the deck of the pirate ship. There was a part of him that wished these thugs had just shot him when they'd boarded the old shrimper. At least that way he'd have been spared being humiliated in front of Rick and Rose. He would also have skipped seeing the treasure they'd worked so hard for being stolen right in front of them.

"Charlie!" Lasorda shouted up to the thug on the boat near Humphrey. "Tie that limping bum up and get down here. I need everyone hauling this loot."

"Right, boss," Charlie said.

Charlie glared at Humphrey. "Don't move, old man."

*Old man?* Humphrey thought. "It wasn't that long ago I was shooting down German aces over Belgium, junior."

"And now all you can do is shoot off your mouth. And you can stop doing that right now before I close it for you permanent like."

*If my hands weren't tied, and you didn't have a gun...*Humphrey looked the muscular man over as the thug entered the cockpit *...and I was a bit more in shape, there'd be a lesson being taught right now.*

The thug returned with another short length of rope. He tied it off around the one that bound Humphrey's wrists together, and then lashed them and Humphrey tight to the boat's railing.

"Sit tight, old man." He gave Humphrey an annoying pinch on the cheek. Hatred roiled inside the pilot.

Charlie went to the bow and climbed down to the rocks below. He made his way up the pirate boat's stern and then went below decks. From the pirate ship's deck, Rick turned his head so the thug keeping an eye on him couldn't see his face and gave Humphrey a concerned look. Humphrey nodded and flashed Rick an awkward thumbs up from his bound hands. Rick nodded and began to speak to Rose.

Humphrey looked down at the rope binding him to the ship's railing. "Well, Charlie, you weren't no Boy Scout, were you? Because this kinda knot would make a tenderfoot blush."

Humphrey *had* been a Boy Scout, and he could see what this bozo had tied wasn't a square knot, but two half hitches. The former was tough to untie under a load, the latter was not. Of course, he couldn't reach the knot with his fingers to untie it, but by twisting the old rope back and forth there was a damn good chance he could get the thing to untie itself. At a minimum he could get it loose enough that he could grab it with his teeth and untie it the rest of the way. He just had to make sure none of Lasorda's men caught wind of what he was doing.

Humphrey began to twist and turn his wrists within his bindings, inching the rope back and forth a fraction of an inch. All the while he stared ahead at the pirate ship, ready to stop the instant one of Lasorda's men, or Lasorda himself, took notice of what he was doing.

Rick watched as Charlie climbed aboard the pirate ship and stood next to Sal. That put Lasorda and his whole crew onboard the *Avarice*. That was actually a good thing, as it left Humphrey unattended.

Rose whispered to Rick. "Now what?"

"Humphrey's our wild card," Rick said. "He'll make a move."

"We're relying on Humphrey? Thanks for moving me from the worried column to the despondent column."

Rick hoped Humphrey would use this chance to do…well, to do *something* now that he wasn't being so closely watched. Getting control of Lasorda's boat would be a good first step. That boat was their only chance of getting across the caiman-ridden cove.

Lasorda returned to the upper deck with Virginia right behind him. Rick gritted his teeth. He had always considered betrayal unconscionable. He rarely trusted anyone but Rose, and Virginia was Exhibit A in his case for why.

Lasorda had a handful of gold coins. He showed them to the others in his open palm. "Have you ever seen so much gold in one place? I'm gonna need to build myself a vault for it all."

"You won't get away with this," Damien said.

"Boy, if I had a nickel for every time someone said that to me," Lasorda laughed. "I still wouldn't have as much money as I have right now!"

Lasorda tossed the gold coins down on the deck between Rick and Virginia. They landed with a chorus of high-pitched pings. "Here, this is as close as *you're* gonna get to them."

The gangster looked over the railing and down to the main deck. "Charlie, gimme your heater. I want your hands full of treasure. You and Sal go below."

Charlie tossed his tommy gun up to Lasorda, who caught it in mid-air. He passed the machine gun over to Virginia. "Sweetheart, you keep an eye on these two. I don't need them messing up the works."

"Got it," Virginia said.

Lasorda and his men went back below deck. Rick tensed to make a rush for Virginia.

She leveled the weapon at him. "You don't want to do that. I'll cut you both down. While you might want to die trying to be a hero, I know you don't want that to happen to Rose."

"Don't be so sure about that," Rose said. "I was the one who talked him into trusting you. You'd double-cross us so a gangster could make you rich?"

Virginia picked a few gold coins up off the deck. "I couldn't care less about your stupid gold and jewels. You think treasure hunting is why I'm here?"

"It sure seems that way," Rose said.

Virginia tucked the coins in her pocket. "I'm here because Justinia was my family. Wrongly accused of being a volunteer for Blackbeard. Her spirit has been trapped here for two hundred years. Now I've found her and will bring her home."

"In what?" Rick said. "Don't tell me. This is some kind of genie-in-a-lamp thing?"

Virginia's grip on the tommy gun tightened at the insult. "She is tethered to her remains. Lasorda and his men will take the treasure out of here, and I'll take her body in one of the treasure cases."

Rick looked closely at the forward mast. Indeed, the witch's corpse wasn't pinned there anymore, and a box sat at the mast's base.

"She will come home," Virginia continued, "and there she will teach me all the secrets of witchcraft, of the spells lost to time or destroyed by the unbelievers."

"I disliked you as a turncoat," Rick said, "but as an evil witch, I despise you."

"And people like you will be the first to see what happens with the power Justinia shares with me."

"Lasorda won't let you get back to the mainland alive any more than he'll let us," Rose said.

Virginia pulled a medallion with a pentagram on it up from the front of her shirt. "The difference there is that I have Justinia's protection."

Countless hours of reading players at poker tables told Rick Virginia wasn't as confident of that boast as she tried to make it sound. It was like she had three-of-a-kind and really hoped she had the winning hand. Knowing even Virginia wasn't certain of her safety made him even more uncertain of his own and Rose's.

"You're going to trust your life to some untried witchcraft?" Rick said.

"Untried? What do you think kept us safe in the chart house all night? My spell. What do you think drove off the iguana attack at the pond? Another of my spells. And my spell to call the sea wasps would have killed you all if you hadn't blown up the side of the cavern."

Lasorda stepped back onto the main deck. His pockets so bulged with treasure that he had to waddle to keep his balance. "You Sinclairs delivered the motherlode, here. I'm gonna be set for life. And this secret island? It's gonna become my smuggler's paradise, just like it was for Blackbeard. Virginia, you use that heater in your hands as an invitation for the Sinclairs to go into the hold and bring this loot to the deck."

Lasorda lowered himself over the side and began to work his way down the rock pile. Charlie and Sal came up out of the hold, struggling with one of the metal treasure boxes. The two men were built like boxers, so if they were having a tough time of it, it had to be heavy as hell. Rick couldn't help but wonder how much treasure was inside.

The men made it to the pirate ship's railing just as Lasorda made it to the ladder at his ship's bow.

Suddenly, the top of the box at the forward mast blew off with a boom. A cloud of green mist billowed from the container and a shockwave that stank of sulfur and burned hair rolled out over Rick and through the cavern. Rose staggered. Rick caught her and only sliding into the ship's wheel kept them from falling. Damien wrapped his arms around the forward railing and held on.

Virginia was not so lucky. Her feet slipped out from under her on the slick deck. She landed flat on her back and the tommy gun spun away from her and smacked against the deck's far railing.

The cloud over the box dissipated and left behind a green-tinged form that was the spitting image of the corpse that had been tied to the mast. But this apparition was translucent, and its clothes were no longer faded and torn. The biggest difference were the eyes, which burned bright red like two blacksmith's coals. The mouth of the witch's spirit twisted into a snarl.

"No one takes treasure bought with my blood!" she cried out.

She cupped her hands together and a sphere of red light flared to life between them. She released her hands and the light split into a dozen individual beams. Each beam struck the skull of one of the skeletons that lay upon the deck. The bones around each skull rattled against the petrified wood.

Charlie and Sal dropped their box on the deck and it landed with a crash. The lid broke off and revealed a sparkling cache of gold and jewels. Lasorda hung frozen halfway up the cargo net, transfixed by the sight of the floating apparition. Frankie got to the top of the staircase from the hold carrying a pile of gold coins cradled in the extended front of his shirt. He saw the floating witch, stopped, and let go of his shirt. Gold coins rained down back into the hold like a slot machine payout.

Then the skeletons of the dead pirates rearticulated and rose to their feet, each brandishing the weapon it had died carrying.

"We need to get off this ship," Rick said.

# CHAPTER TWENTY-FOUR

Lasorda's men recovered from their shock. Charlie and Sal, near the railing, drew pistols from their belts. Frankie dropped down into the hold and reappeared with a tommy gun.

The witch floated over the stub of the mast. Like someone working marionettes, she twisted hands and fingers and in response, the pirate skeletons headed for the men with their bladed weapons held high. Half went for Frankie at the entrance to the hold, and half toward Sal and Charlie by the railing.

Damien scrambled across the deck and scooped up the tommy gun. Virginia sat up. Damien pounced on her and smacked her in the jaws with the butt stock. Virginia slumped to the deck and did not move.

Below them, the men let loose a fusillade of bullets at the skeleton attackers. Most of the rounds passed through the empty space between the bones. One round struck a skull and exploded it into a snowstorm of chips. The skeleton collapsed to the ground.

The rest of the resurrected continued their step-by-step advance on the men. As they did, the bits of the downed skeleton's shattered skull reassembled, as if a film of its explosion ran in reverse. When it was again whole, the skeleton returned to its feet.

"They're not going to stop those skeletons," Damien said.

"Then we're going to have to stop the witch," Rick said. "Virginia said the soul resided in her body, and she was taking the body back home. Destroy the body, destroy the witch?"

"Worth a shot. Beats waiting for those skeletons to chop us up."

"Everything I need is below decks," Rick said. "You keep Rose safe."

"What?" Rose said. "I'm going with you."

"This is a one-man job, Rosie. Sit tight and I'll be right back."

Rick was up and running across the deck before she could let loose the furious objection he was sure she was about to deliver. He hopped over the unconscious Virginia and bounded down the steps.

He headed straight into the melee. Pirate skeletons and Damien's men were locked in combat. Frankie swung his weapon by the barrel and was parrying the swipes of the swords of two skeletons at the entrance to the hold. At the railing, Sal fended off blows from a skeleton's cutlass with a big gold platter he must have taken from the box of loot. Charlie was taking aim, sometimes pointblank, at skulls and blasting them. But the collapsed skeletons were reassembling even faster after each shot.

Rick crouched down, dashed down the steps and into the partially collapsed cabin. There beside the bits of the cannons, he found what he was looking for: the keg of gunpowder. He picked it up and shook it. It wasn't empty, but it wasn't anywhere near full. There wasn't time to scrape open a different, full keg. He hoped it had enough inside for what he intended to do.

Now, he had to get to the bow. He turned back to the steps. A skeleton with a long sword blocked his way. It raised the weapon and headed for Rick.

The collapse of the cabin had opened a hole in the deck that looked just wide enough for him to get through. With the keg of explosives under one arm, he lowered himself through the hole. The deck's jagged edge raked his savaged, naked back and sent bolts of pain through his body. Holding on with his free arm, he realized he could not see the deck below, couldn't gauge the distance, didn't know if he'd twist an ankle or worse landing on a treasure box.

The skeleton made it to the hole. It sent the sword down toward Rick's arm like a guillotine.

He let go and dropped as the blade clanged against the solid deck. Rick landed in a pile of coins. While individually hard, collectively they were forgiving. The coins slid and shifted as he landed, absorbing the impact. As they slipped under his feet, he toppled over. An image of a spark setting off the spilled contents of the keg sent a flash of terror through him. He hugged the keg tight and aimed a shoulder at the deck. He struck the petrified wood hard. Tendons there stretched and snapped.

But the keg didn't spill. He pulled himself up, and shifted the keg to under his remaining good shoulder. His left one was going to hurt like hell pretty soon. He needed to be done before that.

He ran along the length of the hold to the forward stairs. He vaulted up the steps and into the foc'sle, then turned to look out the doorway to the main deck.

The fight was going badly for Lasorda's men. Frankie lay by the opening to the hold in at least two pieces and a skeleton with a bloody cutlass stood over his corpse. At the other end of the deck, Sal and Charlie looked like they were at the center of a skeleton swarm. Cutlass blades clanged against whatever treasures the men could raise in their flagging defense. The witch floated above it all, focused on the stern of the ship. She cackled in glee and redirected the skeleton at the cargo hold opening. It turned and began to move to where Damien and Rose now stood on the raised deck by the ship's wheel.

The terrified look on Rose's face filled Rick with fury at the witch. Her skeletons were not going to touch his wife.

A skeleton launched its cutlass in a wide, upward sweep and sent the gold plate in Charlie's hands flying over the side of the ship. Another skeleton took advantage of the opening and thrust a dagger into Charlie's chest. He cried out and then his scream reduced to an agonized gurgle as he sank to the deck. All the skeletons turned their attention to embattled Sal.

When Sal fell, the witch would send the whole skeleton crew after Rose and Damien. Rick was out of time.

Rick pulled the match box from his pocket and extracted a match. He clamped his teeth around the wooden end. Then he burst from the foc'sle with the gunpowder keg under one arm and dashed for the open box at the base of the mast. Sliding in like he was stealing second base, the soles of his shoes slammed the box against the railing. He glanced in to see the witch's corpse piled up inside.

The crash below her caught the witch's attention. She looked down and the glow of her red eyes seemed to burn holes through Rick's body. He'd never felt such a paralyzing fear. The witch spun one hand in a circle over her head.

Sal screamed and then went silent. The clack of bone against the deck grew louder and a skeleton came running to the witch's defense.

At the far end of the ship, Rose screamed, "Rick!"

The sound of his stricken wife jump started his body. Rick dumped the keg upside down into the box. He bit down harder on the match, then with a twist of his neck, he ran the match head against the box's edge. A flame sparked to life and he spat the match into the box. Then he dropped to his back on the cold deck and covered his ears.

The gunpowder exploded and the sides of the metal box sent the blast straight up. Burning bits of cloth and bone pierced the witch's apparition like buckshot through a curtain. Each flaming piece ripped a black hole through the witch and sailed off into space. The edges of each hole caught fire.

The look on the witch's face shifted from fury to panic. She jerked back and slapped at the expanding, blazing holes in her body. But the flames continued to expand. The rest of her body began to fade away. She rotated her face to the ceiling and let out a horrific, animal-like wail. The sweeping flames consumed the last of her and she vanished.

The skeletons throughout the ship collapsed, as if their marionette strings had been cut. Damien had the tommy gun raised, ready to crash the butt stock into an attacking skeleton when it disassembled. Damien and Rose smiled with relief. Nothing on the ship's main deck moved. Lasorda's men had been no match for the skeletons.

Rick looked into the box and saw only shards of bone and blackened cloth. He hoped whatever little was left wasn't enough to harbor the soul of the evil witch. Rick made his way back to the stern.

As he hit the top of the steps, Rose rushed to him and wrapped him in a bear hug. "You big idiot. What did you think you were doing?"

"Saving my wife, being a hero. You know, the usual."

She slapped him on the back of the head. "That's for not telling me your plan."

Rick wasn't about to confess that he'd barely had one when he rushed off. This was not the time to admit this was a fake-it-until-I-figure-it-out plan. "Fine. Next time a witch is sending reanimated skeletons to kill us, I will run all my plans through you."

"Deal."

Something crashed down on the deck. All three of them looked over. A rock that had to weigh a hundred pounds sat across the opening to the hold. New cracks ran through the petrified wood in all directions from it.

"Where the—" Rick looked up at the ceiling just as another rock came plummeting down. It hit near the stub of the main mast and left it cocked.

"I think that blast weakened the ceiling," Damien said. "The more of it that falls, the more of it is going to fall."

"Then we'd better get out of its way," Rick said.

# CHAPTER TWENTY-FIVE

Humphrey stood bound to the railing of Lasorda's boat, spellbound by the chaos that had erupted on the pirate ship. It was hard to believe he'd watched resurrected skeletons, what looked like a floating ghost, and finally a blast that brought it all to an end.

Something splashed in the water beside the boat. His first thought was of a caiman on the attack, but when he looked down all he saw were concentric rings of ripples. Then something clanked on the bow. He turned just in time to duck a softball-sized rock that whizzed by his head. Across the cavern, other rocks dropped from the ceiling. It seemed like whatever had exploded on the pirate ship and stopped the witch had started something that could be even more deadly.

"Humphrey!" Rick shouted from the pirate ship deck. "We're coming over. Hold tight."

Still tied to the railing, he didn't have any other choice. "Roger that!"

He went back to work untying the cheesy knot that held him to the boat. Then Lasorda's head popped up over the bow railing. The lowlife coward hadn't died with his men. Humphrey expected nothing less.

Humphrey worked the ropes harder. The friction began to heat his already chafed wrists. He knew rope burn would be the least of his problems if the gangster got to him before he was free.

Lasorda rolled over the railing and landed on the bow. Being a gangland boss apparently hadn't kept him in shape. He pulled himself up and staggered back toward Humphrey and the pilothouse. Sweat poured down his beet-red face. His pockets bulged with what

Humphrey assumed was pirate treasure. Another big rock fell on the bow and bounced off into the water.

Off the bow, Damien, Rick, and Rose climbed down the rocks from the pirate ship. Lasorda was too busy saving his own skin to even notice.

"The roof is collapsing," Humphrey said. "You can't just leave them there."

"Oh yeah?" Lasorda said. "Watch me."

He pushed past Humphrey and into the pilothouse. Humphrey knew he had to buy some time to give the others a chance to start climbing the ladder.

"You're all the same," Humphrey said. "All you big bullies-turned-criminal. When the danger gets personal, y'all turn yellow as summertime piss."

Lasorda began to throw switches in the pilothouse to get the engines restarted. "Why don't you shut up before I shut you up?"

"You couldn't do it. Your womanly arms barely pulled your fat butt up the rope ladder. You've had the hired help do the hard work so long, you don't remember how. Don't embarrass yourself by trying."

"For someone defenseless and tied to a railing, you've got a big mouth."

"For someone supposedly such a big-time gangster, I'm guessing you've got a pretty small--"

Humphrey didn't get to finish the insult. With a frustrated roar, Lasorda charged out of the pilothouse. He balled a fist and sent it crashing into Humphrey's face. The man might be out of shape, but he still packed a hell of a punch. The impact sent Humphrey sideways. The bindings on his wrist went tight and the next thing he knew, he was sitting beside the railing with his hands up over his head. Stars swirled before his eyes.

"How'd those womanly arms feel, Mr. Smart Ass? You're lucky I don't have the time to kill you now."

Lasorda returned to the pilothouse and went back to starting up the boat. Down below, water splashed against the hull. Humphrey glanced down to see that caimans now infested the water. It looked like he wasn't the only one who wanted the boat to stay in place.

Lasorda pressed a button and the engine starter whirled somewhere below decks.

Humphrey looked up at the bindings that were now over his head. Lasorda had done him a favor. The knot had loosened and was now upside down. One loop of the rope hung down, begging Humphrey to pull the knot open the rest of the way.

Lasorda cursed at the cranking engine and yanked a few controls back and forth. The engine coughed once but did not catch.

Humphrey reached up and bit one loop of the knot with his teeth. He snapped his head back and forth until the rope's end worked free.

Lasorda pulled a choke button all the way out. The engines roared to life like a pair of caged tigers. Lasorda slammed a fist against the dashboard and cheered.

Humphrey yanked the binding rope free. In a flash, he was up on his feet. He barreled into the pilothouse just as Lasorda dropped the engines into reverse. Humphrey lowered a shoulder and hit Lasorda in the side like in his old high school football playing days. He carried Lasorda across the pilothouse and out the open door on the other side. Humphrey brushed the ship's wheel and left it spinning behind them.

He and Lasorda hit the railing on the side of the deck. Their combined weight and momentum were too much for the wood to handle. It snapped in the middle and both men went over the edge. Thrashing caimans waited below.

Lasorda plummeted to the water with a high-pitched scream. He hit the surface and a caiman instantly pulled him under. Humphrey followed him over the side. The open maw of another hungry caiman waited to catch him.

Then he jerked to a stop, suspended by his arms in midair. Humphrey looked up to see that the remains of the railing had caught the binding that lashed his wrists together. Now he hung with his feet over water that churned with caimans.

He grabbed the railing with his hands. He tried to swing his feet back up on the deck. The spare tire around his midsection thwarted him.

Like a kid trying to get a swing moving, Humphrey rocked his legs back and forth, building the momentum he needed to reach the deck. The skin on his palms burned with each twist, and he imagined silver dollar-sized blisters forming on each.

His arm muscles burned and ropes dug into his wrists. He wasn't going to be able to do this much longer.

With one last mighty effort, he swung his body upward and his feet landed on the boat. He worked his body up and forward until his back was on the deck. Then he slid the rope off the broken railing and sat up.

There was a loud crash and the boat shook like a struck gong.

The stern of the spinning boat had slammed into part of the cavern. The impact sent Humphrey sliding against the pilothouse. The entire ship shuddered as one propeller disintegrated against solid rock. Another large rock dropped from the ceiling and struck the bow. This one crashed through the deck.

Humphrey realized this ship wasn't going to last long at this rate. He jumped to his feet and entered the pilothouse. A rock hit the starboard windscreen and shattered it. With his bound hands, Humphrey made an awkward shift of the engine controls from reverse to forward, then he labored to turn the wheel, having to use his whole body to get it to move. The boat edged away from the cavern wall.

But the damage was done. From below in the engine room came a repeating slap of metal on metal. Humphrey imagined a driveshaft twisted by the prop hitting stone. He hit the stop button for the starboard engine.

He was too late. Shearing metal screamed from down below, followed by an explosive boom and a shudder that seemed to rock the ship down to its keel. There was no way that story was going to have a happy ending.

Humphrey nudged the boat back into position behind the pirate ship. More falling rock peppered the water. A boulder dropped and struck the pirate ship amidships, sending out bits of petrified wood in all directions.

Rick, Rose, and Damien stood halfway down the rock pile, watching for and dodging bits of cavern ceiling. As soon as Humphrey bumped the bow against the shore, they scrambled down for the boat. The deck soon blocked Humphrey's view.

But they weren't the only ones heading for the boat. The caimans seemed to have sensed fresh food ashore. Half-submerged in the water, they raced up both sides of the ship's hull.

Humphrey left the pilothouse and looked over the starboard side. At the bow, Rick steadied the ladder as Rose started a quick climb. Rick followed and Damien was literally right on his heels, the top of Damien's head smacking the bottom of Rick's shoes.

That was all Humphrey needed to know. He jumped back into the pilothouse and threw the ship into reverse. More unhappy mechanical noises came from below, and Humphrey slid the controls back to neutral. The ship inched away from the shore under a shower of ceiling stone.

Humphrey popped out of the pilothouse again to check on his friends. Rose was at the railing, which put Rick about six feet beneath it. Damien was a bit over halfway up.

An enormous caiman headed for the bow like a torpedo. Other smaller caimans splashed out of its way. It reached the base of the ladder and jumped for Damien. It missed his foot by inches, but got a solid bite on the rope ladder.

The caiman dropped back to the water. The rope ladder stretched, but was never designed to handle this much weight. The ladder tore in half, right above the rung that Damien grasped.

Rick lowered one of his feet down. Damien let go of the ladder and grabbed Rick's ankle with both hands.

Rick's muscles bulged with the strain. "Rosie!" he choked out.

Rose dropped to the deck and grabbed Rick's wrists. Rick raised his foot to the tattered ladder's last rung, and Damien grabbed hold of the ladder. Rose pulled at Rick, and he climbed up onto the deck. Damien followed him.

"Yahoo!" Humphrey shouted as he raised his bound wrists over his head.

Then looking past his friends on the bow, he noticed something that made his heart sink.

Virginia stood on the shore at the stern of the pirate ship, her face contorted in fury. Around her neck, a medallion glowed the same color green as the witch's spirit.

# CHAPTER TWENTY-SIX

There was no way in hell that Virginia was going to let any of these people leave this island alive.

She'd worked her whole adult life building on the research of generations of her family. She'd suffered under Lasorda's heavy thumb, chased down artifacts in miserable locations, and had now almost been killed just as she'd finally arrived to unlock the lost secrets of witchcraft for herself through Justinia.

Then these idiots screwed it up: Lasorda and his trigger-happy henchmen, Damien and his sad crew of thieves. But the top spot on this list went to Rick and Rose Sinclair. Rick had just destroyed Justinia's bones. That meant the witch's soul wouldn't cross over to a better plane of existence, but instead had been dispersed, forever sentenced to an impotent, incoherent state. The Sinclairs had dismissed the power of witchcraft from the first moment she met them.

Now they would experience that power very personally.

The restored medallion around her neck glowed green with residual power from Justinia's spirit. With this, she would supercharge the spell around this island and have every creature converge on the trespassers at once.

She scooped a sharp rock from the ground and slashed both her palms. When the blood began to flow, she pressed the medallion between both hands. She spoke an ancient incantation, and the green glow became dazzlingly bright. Shafts of light spit from between the fingers of her hands. They were so powerful they reached the walls of the cavern.

The medallion grew so hot that her blood sizzled and dried. Virginia smelled her flesh burning, felt the painful blistering of her skin. But a lust for vengeance kept her hands together. She began the protection incantation Justinia had used centuries ago that set the creatures on their murderous paths, and more specifically now, to tear to pieces anyone with pirate treasure. With her power added to it, the four on the boat would never escape.

Virginia finished the chant. The beams from between her fingers rotated across the cavern walls until they rested on the symbols the pirates had carved there long ago. The symbols flashed to life in the same bright green of the medallion.

Her spell was working.

The water suddenly teemed with caimans. They thrashed the water into a frothy mass. Bodies and tails pounded the side of the ship. The four retreated to the pilothouse. Virginia grinned. There would be nowhere they could hide.

At the water's edge, two caimans surfaced and crawled ashore in her direction. Virginia raised an eyebrow. These two should be attacking the ship.

She concentrated harder, trying to send the message out again to kill the ones stealing Blackbeard's treasure. The medallion glowed even brighter.

The caimans roared in unison and charged her. Virginia released the medallion and backed up. She stumbled against the rocks and fell on her side. A lump in her pocket pressed into her hip.

Her eyes went wide as she remembered what that lump was. She reached into her pocket and pulled out the gold coin she'd scooped off the deck after Lasorda had thrown it down.

In the mirrored surface, she saw the open jaws of one of the caimans.

# CHAPTER TWENTY-SEVEN

Rose watched horrified and transfixed as the caimans dashed up the pile of stones at the pirate ship's stern. Virginia lay defenseless on the rocks and screamed in fright.

The first one to Virginia grabbed her with the tip of its snout and tossed her up in the air. The creature opened its mouth to catch her, but the second caiman crashed into it and sent it sideways. The second caiman caught the shrieking Virginia and swallowed her whole.

With the sound like a thunderclap, a great split opened in the ceiling above the pirate ship. Whatever magic Virginia had sent coursing through the cavern walls must have been more than the structure could stand. The previous sprinkle of stones became a hellish hailstorm of black rock across the cavern.

Rose, Rick, and Damien retreated to the relatively safer pilothouse. Rocks rattled against the roof and bounced off the bow. One bounced high and smacked into the forward glass, leaving a spiderweb of cracks behind.

Damien hip-checked Humphrey away from the controls. "You did good for a flyboy, but this is a sailor's job now."

Humphrey raised his bound wrists. "And just imagine if I'd used two hands. But maybe you should take it from here."

Damien slammed the boat into reverse and went to full throttle.

More and larger rocks pounded the boat. One struck the top of the pilothouse and buckled the wood over Rose's head. Another crashed into the bow and punched through the deck, leaving behind a ragged hole two feet wide.

With only one screw turning, the boat wanted to veer hard to port. Damien fought at the wheel to try and keep her heading out of the cavern. The rocky cascade had sent the caimans swimming for safety, but the same falling rock created depth charge-like splashes up along the sides of the boat. Over the pirate ship, the entire cavern roof rumbled.

The boat exited the cavern and entered the full daylight of the cove. Rose felt like she'd been reborn.

From off the bow came a thundering crash. From the top down, the remains of the old volcano imploded, collapsing into itself. The force sent a cloud of black grit and dust out of the cavern's mouth. It sandblasted the bow of the boat and pockmarked the windscreens. As the cloud settled, Damien backed the engine down and leaned against the wheel.

Her adrenaline rush backed off and suddenly Rose felt dead tired.

Humphrey clapped Damien on the shoulder. "Couldn't have done no better myself."

"Happy to oblige." Damien checked the clinometer on the control panel. It showed a five-degree list to starboard.

Humphrey looked sheepish. "I mighta smacked her against a rock a bit, tussling with Lasorda."

"I'll check below." Damien left the pilothouse and went down below decks.

Rick gave Rose a hug. "Are you okay?"

"Just the usual bumps and bruises that seem part and parcel to any trip you plan."

"Someday we'll look back on this and laugh."

"Because your adventures will drive us crazy. We'll be in an asylum laughing at everything."

Rick went to work untying Humphrey's hands. "Good work handling Lasorda."

"He underestimated me."

"Lots of people do."

"Those caimans didn't hesitate to attack Virginia," Rose said. "As someone trying to help the witch, you'd think they'd be on her side."

"The witch's spell was to have the animals protect the treasure," Rick said. "Remember when Virginia put some gold pieces in her pocket on the ship? If she still carried them, the caimans weren't going to let her leave."

"The caimans out here didn't start to attack the boat until Lasorda arrived with pockets full of loot," Humphrey said. "And after they killed him, they backed off and turned their focus to all of you."

"Even if the caimans weren't out for blood defending the treasure," Rick said, "we couldn't get it now with the entire volcano collapsed on top of it. That should mean that the murderous creatures on this island might leave us paupers alone."

Damien ran back up on deck. "We have a problem. The starboard drive shaft shattered and we're taking on water fast. The bilge pump is fighting a losing battle and this boat won't go far."

"That's not our only problem," Rose said. "Looks like our caiman theory is wrong."

She pointed back to the collapsed cavern. In the water between it and the boat, several caimans were headed straight for them.

# CHAPTER TWENTY-EIGHT

With visions of Virginia's gruesome death still horribly fresh in his mind, Rick didn't want to think about he and Rose riding a sinking ship down among a pack of caimans. "Damien, you need to get us to shore before this tub sinks."

"So we can get eaten by giant iguanas?" Rose said.

"Giant iguanas?" Humphrey said.

"You missed out on so much fun," Rick said.

"Humphrey," Damien said. "Did Lasorda damage my *cher bâteau*?"

"No," Humphrey said. "He boarded it and then y'all blasted the volcano wall to smithereens. He dragged me to this boat and we went straight over."

"Then that's how we're getting out of here."

Damien went to the controls and throttled up the remaining engine. He spun the boat around and pointed it at the shrimper off in the cove. The bow knifed through the water and left a white, V-shaped wake. But Rick could see that the boat was now listing much more, and definitely riding lower in the water.

Rose kept a close watch on the caimans across the stern. "They aren't gaining on us, but they're still coming."

"But we aren't taking anything," Humphrey said.

"Maybe these ones are just hungry," Damien said.

"Just our luck," Rick said. "Eating Lasorda and Virginia gave them a taste for humans."

The boat closed on the rusty old shrimper. Damien's boat bobbed at anchor, serene in the face of the swimming monsters and dying ship roaring toward it.

Rick had been hesitant to get aboard the rust bucket when they'd left. Now he couldn't board it fast enough.

"Rick," Damien said. "You get yourself up on the bow. When I come up alongside my boat, jump over carrying that line on the bow cleat. Then you keep the boats close until everyone gets over."

"Will do."

Rick left the pilothouse and went up to the bow. A line about twenty feet long was tied off to the bow cleat. He picked up the coils and grabbed the deck railing on the port side.

The shrimper came up fast. Rick had to keep leaning more into the port side railing as the starboard side of the boat kept tilting toward the water. A glance back over the stern confirmed that several caimans were still in hot pursuit. Even with Damien running the boat wide open, Rick had a bad feeling they were going to be cutting it too close.

The starboard side of the shrimper came up fast. Just when Rick was certain they were going to ram the tired boat head on, Damien slammed the engine into reverse and cut the wheel hard to starboard. The ship heeled even further to starboard and Rick had to grab the railing with both hands to keep from sliding down into the cove.

Then the boat righted itself at a full stop. The two boats floated about a foot away from each other, side by side and bow to bow. Rick shouldn't have doubted Damien's seamanship. He hopped across the small gap onto the shrimper with the bow line in hand. Lasorda's boat began to settle starboard-side low again in an instant.

He turned to see the caimans bearing down on the pair of boats. "Hurry!" he called back.

Humphrey and Rose came charging up to the bow. When they got there, Humphrey stepped aside and motioned Rose to go.

"Ladies first."

"Don't tell me there's a southern gentleman in there somewhere."

"There's a gentleman in all Southerners, ma'am."

Rick pulled the boats a bit closer. Rose jumped across. She landed and teetered on the shrimper's deck. Rick grabbed her with his free hand. She fell against him, gave him a quick hug, and went to the stern of the boat.

The sinking boat lurched even further away from the shrimper and now began to settle stern down as well. Humphrey pulled himself over the boat's railing and balanced on the edge of where the deck met the hull. He was several feet above the shrimper's deck, and now also several feet away from it.

"This is going to hurt," he said.

He crouched and then jumped down to the boat. Humphrey landed beside Rick with a thud and a groan. He dropped to his knees and grabbed his bad ankle.

"That wasn't what the doctor ordered," he said through gritted teeth.

Rose helped him to his feet and he leaned on her shoulder for support.

"Go back and get this thing fired up," Rick said. "As soon as Damien gets aboard, we need to make for open water at full speed."

"Aye, aye." Humphrey gave him a half-assed salute and then Rose helped him hobble back to the stern.

The caimans were now just yards from Lasorda's boat. Unlike Damien's piloted approach, they showed no signs of slowing down. Damien climbed out of the pilothouse just as the first of the reptiles hit the boat. The force threw the boat sideways and into the shrimper. Metal clanged against metal and the shrimper's hull shook. The old boat rolled to port and Rick lost his footing. The bow line slipped from his hands and he gripped the railing to keep from sliding across the deck.

The shock of the caimans strike sent Damien down flat on his chest. The second caiman arrived and stuck its long snout over the sinking stern gunwale. A huge, clawed foot came out of the water and slammed down onto the deck. Wood splintered as the claws bit into the boat.

The extra weight sent the boat's bow skyward. The hull rose so far up that it exposed a mass of seaweed and barnacles beneath the boat's waterline. Damien grabbed the side railing and began to pull himself up to the bow.

As the shrimper righted itself, the bow line snaked away across the pockmarked deck. Rick dropped to the deck and grabbed it. He jumped to his feet and tried to hold the line fast.

Damien scrambled up the canted deck using the railing like a ladder. The caiman brought its other foot up onto the boat and the hull moaned under the added stress. The bow of Lasorda's boat rose higher as the stern sank. The gap between the boats grew to several feet.

The shrimper's engines fired up with a roar and a cloud of black smoke belched from the stern. The bow line slipped in Rick's sweaty hands and delivered a sizzling rope burn. He clenched his teeth and held tight. If he let go, Damien would never make it. He was only two-thirds of the way up the sinking boat.

The caiman kept crawling up the deck, sideways step by sideways step with its front feet. Wood and metal crunched with each footfall. It reached the pilothouse and hissed.

Damien made it to the bow and stood up, wobbling behind the railing. The rope to the bow ran beside one of his feet, stretched tight as a bridge cable. Rick's arm muscles burned and he wasn't sure how much longer he could hold on.

"Jump!" he shouted.

Damien stepped over the railing and balanced on the now near vertical joint between the deck and the hull. It was then that Rick noticed the lumps in Damien's pants pockets. The greedy man had taken some of Blackbeard's spoils after all. No wonder the caimans were still after them.

"Damn it," he said. "You have treasure in your pockets? Get rid of it and stop this attack."

"Can't go home empty handed," he said with an avaricious smile. "One jump and then we're all on our way home and at least one of us is rich."

Damien crouched and then sprang up and across, aiming for the shrimper's deck. His smile widened as he closed on his boat.

As he was halfway there, it seemed to Rick that everything went into slow motion. Another caiman exploded vertically out of the water right beneath him. Its jaws opened wide and for a split-second Damien was suspended between a V of sharp, white teeth. Then the jaws snapped closed, leaving only his head exposed. His smile turned to shock.

The caiman landed sideways between the boats and sent a wall of water across both ships' decks. Rick let the rope go just as Lasorda's boat pointed straight at the sky. The other caiman crawled up onto the bow. It stared at Rick as the boat slipped beneath the waves. The caiman sank with it until only its eyes remained above water, then those disappeared as well.

The world went back to normal speed. Several large bubbles rose and burst where Lasorda's ship had gone down. Then the water returned to its calm imitation of a tropical paradise.

“Rick,” Humphrey said, “pull up that anchor. Let’s get out of here.”

Rick went forward and winched up the anchor. As its flukes broke the surface, Humphrey gunned the boat’s engines. He sent it in a wide sweeping turn and then headed straight for the cove’s exit. Rick staggered back to the stern where Rose waited with a relieved look on her face. She wrapped her arms around his neck and kissed him.

He hugged her back.

“That was too close,” she said.

“Damien nearly got us killed. The caimans were after the treasure he had stuffed in his pockets.”

“You think they’ll let us go?” she said.

Rick looked back across the waters of the cove. There wasn’t a caiman to be seen. “Seems like it.”

“You don’t mind if I keep high-tailing it away from this place,” Humphrey said, “just to be sure.”

“Absolutely!” Rick and Rose said together.

The boat passed through the cove entrance and into the blue Caribbean. The island began to recede into the distance.

“You know the course home?” Rick asked Humphrey.

“Not exactly, but I figure if we head north, we’ll hit North America somewhere. And at this point, I ain’t so picky about where.”

“You know, neither am I.”

# CHAPTER TWENTY-NINE

*Six months later.*

Rose looked out from behind the curtains at the crowd on the Charleston auction house floor. The turnout was much better than she'd expected. Every seat was filled, and most were filled by men in suits who had travelled from as far away as Maine. To the left of the stage, the auctioneer prepared himself behind a podium.

Rick stepped up beside her and handed her the final list of items to be auctioned. "All the paperwork is signed. At the end of this auction, we walk away with twenty-five percent of the gross."

The landlord of the Charleston warehouse hadn't had any idea where to turn when the deceased Lasorda missed his rent payment. Lasorda had been paying through a shell company to hide his identity from the authorities, but that had been a dead end for the landlord as well. By law he'd ended up with the unclaimed contents of the warehouse. To get rid of it all, he contracted Rick and Rose, whose business card he came across on top of Virginia's work desk. If everything went according to plan, their commission would make them and Humphrey whole again, with a little left over for their time and trouble.

"I'm surprised at the number and caliber of the people at this auction," Rose said.

"People will come out for a collection of genuine Blackbeard artifacts."

"But most of the stuff in the warehouse wasn't."

"Shh, not so loud."

Rose's eyes narrowed. "What did you do?"

"Me? I may have mentioned to one or two people, completely as a hypothetical, that items in the auction could have been taken from the wreck of the *Queen Anne's Revenge*, but could not be listed as such because of some murky salvage rights."

"That's not true."

"I never said it was. Now what the rumor mill churned my innocent statements into is completely out of my control."

"That's dishonest."

"The auction catalog doesn't claim anything is from the *Queen Anne's Revenge*, and that's what people should use to guide their bidding. If they don't, well, what can I do? And besides, all those stuffed shirts bidding out there are buying for rich people up North who are going to stick whatever it is in their smoking room and never look at it again. At the worst, this is a victimless crime, if it's even a crime at all."

Rose was pretty sure that a crime had been committed somewhere in Rick's little pre-auction performance. Now she just had to hope that no one caught wind of his scheme.

Two hours later, the auction was down to its last item. Backstage, Rick had kept a running count of the total throughout the event. A flurry of bids crisscrossed the room and the gavel fell on a set of dueling pistols. The auctioneer bid all the attendees a goodnight and the room began to empty.

Rick added the price to his list and summed up the total. "Rosie, we did better than break even on this little adventure."

Rose looked at the number. It wasn't large, but it also did not have a minus sign in front of it. "That will keep us afloat for the next few months."

"Just long enough for me to bring in a few more of my unique, can't miss finds."

"You mean *can't sell* finds? Just leave the purchasing to me, please."

Rose flipped through the final auction list and then looked at the catalog. "What happened to the sword?"

"What sword?"

Rose gritted her teeth. Rick's innocent act never sounded the remotest bit innocent. "Eighteenth century rapier, engraved hand guard, single ruby in the handle. *That* sword."

"Ohh, glad you reminded me. Yeah, I made a great pre-sale swap for that."

"Swap? That sword was worth enough to buy a new truck."

"As if we needed one," Rick said. "The point is, I traded up in value, as I always do."

"You'd trade a cow for magic beans if I didn't stop you."

"This time you'll be glad that you didn't. Come see."

Rick led her back to a deserted corner of the auction house. On a table there rested a blocky wood carving of a head at about twice the normal size. The style was Central American, probably Aztec from the face's broad features and the ring of glyphs that ran around the base.

"This," Rick said, like he was introducing royalty to a state dinner, "is from a consignment of artifacts brought back by an expedition deep into the jungles of Mexico. One-of-a-kind, thousands of years old. This will be worth way more than that old sword could be."

Rose picked up the head. It was much heavier than she expected. She examined several sides of it. She set it down and sighed.

"This is a fake. Who did you get this from?"

"Fake? That's solid mahogany. I got it from a friend of mine who has an excellent reputation."

"You don't have friends with excellent reputations. And this is made of pine with a mahogany stain."

"That can't be. That wood is strong as iron. Watch."

Rick took a knife from his pocket and flipped it open. He placed the blade against the side of the head and made a quick downward stroke. A giant shaving of wood curled up in front of the knife, exposing soft, yellow pine behind it.

Rick's jaw sagged. "I can't believe Lefty would cheat me."

"I can't believe someone named Lefty wouldn't."

Rose looked closer at the exposed pine. The grain did not match along the center of the gash, like it had been made of two separate pieces instead of carved from a single block. She took the knife from Rick's hand and wedged it into the seam in the middle. The two pieces were not glued together. She ran the knife blade further down the side and hit something hard. She scraped away the wood in that area and uncovered a contemporary metal hinge.

"That confirms that this carving is a fake," Rick said.

"It also tells that this head conceals something inside it," Rose said.

She ran the knife blade around the edge of the head, scratching the varnish and stain from a seam that went all the way around. She did not find the clasp or lock that held it closed. She set the head back down.

"There has to be a way to open this."

"I have an axe at home."

"We can't risk damaging whatever is hidden inside by using too much force. It isn't a piggy bank."

Rick picked up the head and began to examine it from all angles. "I saw this detective movie once where there was a secret safe behind a painting. The release was hidden in the frame design."

Rick began to squeeze random features on the head.

"Rick, there's no way that—"

Rick pressed the right eye and the right ear at the same time. Something clicked in the carving and the front half of the head popped open.

"Voila," Rick said. "Hollywood to the rescue again,"

He opened the head. In a rectangular hollow in the middle lay a slab of glossy volcanic obsidian. Into it were carved a randomly arranged set of hieroglyphs, with arrows pointing from one glyph to another. Other symbols like a string of Vs and squiggly lines crossed the stone as well.

Rose gingerly removed the slab. It was a fraction of an inch thick and she was afraid it would shatter if she dropped it. No wonder someone had made the head as a decorative case for it.

Taking out the slab revealed a piece of paper that had been hidden beneath it. Rick picked it up and held it alongside the slab. It contained a list of the hieroglyphs and an English translation beside each. The list included Tenochtitlan, Cholula, Cuahnahuac, and Tollocan. The last one on the list was Tezpaluca.

"I knew trading for this was a sure bet," Rick said. "I had a feeling that...whatever that black thing is, was inside waiting to be discovered."

"It's a map," Rose said. "And I recognize some of those names. They're Aztec cities."

Rick stared at her, waiting for more.

"The Aztec were the native people in Mexico when the Spanish arrived, but they had been there for two hundred years before that. They supposedly had a great empire, but many of the cities were lost to the jungle after the empire collapsed."

Rick's eyes lit up. "Didn't the Spanish go there in search of gold and jewels?"

"Especially looking for Tezpaluca," Rose said. "A mythical city dedicated to the Aztec god of the night sky, Tezcatlipoca. The city supposedly had been a great seat of Aztec power, possibly the source of the tales of a city with streets of gold."

"Well, if it's on a map, it must be more than mythical. And if the Spanish never found it, that can only be because Fate has decreed that we're supposed to."

Rose scoffed. "You think the two of us are going to slash our way through the jungle and find a lost city?"

"The two of us? Don't be ridiculous. We'll bring someone who can help with the locals."

"Don't you dare say Humphrey."

"Of course Humphrey. He flies all over Central America, and he speaks Spanish. Plus, he can help with any heavy lifting. We'll give him a cut of what we find. We owe him for nearly getting him killed on Blackbeard's Island."

"It's going to take a lot of verification that this is authentic before I agree to this new wild goose chase."

"I'll start on that as soon as we get home."

"And this time we need an actual plan, not some seat-of-the-pants adventure."

"I excel at planning."

"No you don't. This idea is terrible."

"This idea is spectacular. You just follow my lead, and everything will work out."

To the best of Rose's recollection, every time she'd followed Rick's lead, nothing had worked out as planned. She had a bad feeling this next expedition would be no different.

The End

# AFTERWORD

Rick and Rose have managed to make it home again. There were a few places here where even I was afraid they wouldn't make it. But they have lived to treasure hunt another day. They found, but could not keep, the treasure of Blackbeard the pirate.

How much of his story in this novel is true-to life? Quite a bit, actually.

Likely born as Edward Teach (location in dispute), the future Blackbeard acquired a taste for plunder as a privateer for England during Queen Anne's War. At the end of the war, his legal commission to plunder expired, but he just kept at it.

He commanded his own ship for the first time in 1717. He rechristened the captured ship *Queen Anne's Revenge* and it had a crew of approximately 300 men and between 30 and 40 cannons, depending on the source material. He and his men sailed the Caribbean and the Atlantic coast of North America. He was able to make North Carolina a base of operations by bribing the governor to look the other way.

Blackbeard knew that a fearsome image could tip the battle in his favor, and cultivated one of being a bloodthirsty crazed pirate. He did indeed wrap slow burning lighted fuses in his long hair and beard to intimidate his victims. As in the story, he did have a reputation for inhuman strength and for invincibility, but there was never any claim that witchcraft was the source of either.

By 1718, Blackbeard had amassed a personal fleet of four captured vessels. At this point, the governor of Virginia decided if North Carolina wasn't going to stop this pirate, he would, and he dispatched his own vessels to take out Blackbeard. In the ensuing battle, Blackbeard suffered twenty-five stab wounds and five gunshots before succumbing to his injuries. He was decapitated, and his head hung on the victorious *Ranger's* bowsprit as it sailed back into port.

By his last encounter, Blackbeard was down to only one of his four ships. What happened to one of the others is a bit murky, so it became the *Avarice*, one entombed at Blackbeard's fictional island in the novel.

While there has always been talk about Blackbeard's treasure, it is very unlikely that there ever was any. Blackbeard's crew split the spoils after raids, and pirates were not known to be thrifty or to put a few doubloons away for a rainy day.

The *Queen Anne's Revenge* was not lost in battle, but on a sand bar off the North Carolina coast. In 1938, when the story is set, it had not been found. But in 1996, a private salvage company discovered the wreck. A lot of the artifacts have been salvaged and conserved. There's a splendid display of them at the North Carolina Maritime Museum in Beaufort, and anyone interested in seeing some up close and personal pirate gear should check the museum out.

The flag emblem on the map was one actually flown from Blackbeard's ship. One of the earliest pirate flags used, it depicted a heart dripping blood and a skeleton holding an hourglass and spear. The hope was that the sight of it would intimidate ships to surrender, and it did just that. And while this symbol on the map was the real thing, the witch symbols used throughout the book are straight from my imagination.

All of the Roma witchcraft is just as fictional, although the Roma people do have a very rich culture with ties to mysticism.

On the island, Rick and Rose have to face some seriously dangerous creatures. The first is a giant caiman.

In real life, the black caiman is common in South America. They look most similar to an American alligator, but with much darker coloration. They can grow to about twenty feet, half the size of the monsters on Blackbeard's Island. They will eat anything they can catch, including other caiman, deer, tapirs, anacondas, and wayward farm animals. Their teeth are designed to grab instead of rip, so they drown their catch underwater, then swallow it whole. Several fatal attacks on humans are reported each year in the Amazon region. As Rick would say, helpful safety tip: stay away from caimans.

The second creature encountered are giant iguanas. Iguanas are native to the Caribbean, South and Central America. If you've been to South Florida, you've seen them roaming around, but here they are an invasive species, likely pets that escaped or were set free. In real life they can grow to up to six feet long and weigh 20 pounds. Fearsome as they look, they are herbivores and prefer hibiscus to human flesh. I am told they make good pets, but there's no way I want something in my house longer than I am tall that looks like a Jurassic Park escapee.

The third creature that tries to doom our heroes is a giant sea wasp jellyfish. The real-life versions of these are not to be trifled with. The sea wasp is a box jelly with potent and painful venom that can kill people in as few as three minutes. The sea wasp's transparent, small body has tentacles, which reach up to 10 feet long. Each of the 60 hanging tentacles contain stinging cells called cnidocytes.

Jellyfish join fire ants as one of my most hated species. The good news is sea turtles munch on them, so when you support sea turtles, you get even with jellyfish by proxy. Helpful Hint Number Two: Stay away from sea wasps, and any other types of jellyfish.

When I was noodling the story out, I really wanted to have Rick and Rose find an actual pirate ship. But there was no way to get a reader to suspend disbelief about a wooden ship surviving two centuries. But then while I was at Yellowstone National Park researching the Kathy West Adventure *Ravens of Yellowstone*, I found a way around that. Petrified wood.

Petrified wood is actually fossilized wood. For wood to go through the transformation, first it has to be buried in sediment to be protected from decay. Then, mineral-rich groundwater flows through the sediment. The wood's original plant material is replaced with elements like silica, calcite, and pyrite. The result is a fossil of the original so complete that you can often still make out the details in the bark and wood.

Could this have really happened to the treasure ship? Well, I put most of the needed elements into the story to make it possible. If you want to poo-poo this idea, I'll remind you that you already bought off on three giant monsters, so you have to give me this one.

Thanks go out to my wonderful Beta readers Donna Fitzpatrick, Deb DeAlteriis, and Lucille Bransfield who tasted this meal early and made sure it was not undercooked. I also need to express great appreciation for everyone at Severed Press who through sharp editing and the creation of knock-out covers, turn my stories into something people might want to read.

Seems that Rick has talked Rose into another quest. How's that going to work out? You'll have to wait and see. In the meantime, you can check out my Grant Coleman Adventures series and my Ranger Kathy West Adventures series, also published by Severed Press.

To keep up to date on the progress of new works, my appearance schedule, and even some automotive tips, sign up for my monthly newsletter here. https://landing.mailerlite.com/webforms/landing/i5k2m1

You can also drop by my website https: www.russellrjames.com, look me up on Twitter @RRjames14 or check out my Facebook antics at https://www.facebook.com/russell.r.james/ or the author page at https://www.facebook.com/profile.php?id=100049500016706 . I hope to hear from you soon.

-Russell James

Printed in Great Britain
by Amazon

40717245R00099